The Adventures of Razor and Edge

Russ Crossley

53RD STREET PUBLISHING

Acknowledgement

A word of appreciation must go to Kris Rusch and Dean Smith for their support and encouragement. Without their insight and willingness to share their extensive knowledge of the art and business of writing and publishing it is very likely you would not be holding this book in your hands.

Introduction

This collection is only possible because of a few important people. Someone once said to me publishing is a collaborative business, I believe this is true.

Firstly, I'd like to say special thank you to my wife, Rita. She always believes in me even when I make those occasional slip-ups us guys are wont to make.

Next, I'd like to thank Kris Rusch and Dean Smith two knowledgeable professional writers who go above and beyond, not only for me but also for hundreds of writers across the planet. We are the benefactors of their knowledge, experience, and willingness to help us writers achieve the steady goals necessary to be a success in this business.

And lastly, I'd like to thank my editor, Barbara, for her expertise and helpful suggestions that made the first story in this collection so much better.

In this collection you will find stories reminiscent of the legendary characters of detective fiction, Sherlock Holmes and Dr. Watson, and Nero Wolfe and Archie Goodwin.

I don't claim Razor and Edge are as iconic as these characters. This humble writer intentionally tried to emulate the feel of those stories without trying to copy them, or improve on them.

Those classic character types are legends of crime fiction whose stories I love .

Whether or not I succeeded in my goal in these Razor and Edge stories is up to you, the reader, as it should be.

I hope you enjoy these tales of this quirky detective team and would welcome feedback on my Facebook page by Twitter or through my publishers website http://www.53rdstreetpublishing.com

The Adventures of Razor and Edge

by Russ Crossley

Published by 53rd Street Publishing

Trade paperback ISBN 978-1-927621-36-3

Ebook ISBN 9781465801715

Cover art: © Annkozar | Dreamstime.com

Cover design and interior layout by R. Edgewood
Cover design and layout copyright © 53rd Street
Publishing

Table of Contents

Mirror Image

A Razor and Edge Mystery

1

MURDER IN OUR OWN BACKYARD. Finally.

I eased back into the folds of my lavender covered computer office chair. I sipped my now warm cola; the can set on a coaster on the grey desk next to the keyboard and studied the words I planned to send to our blog.

If it really happened, the murder of a neighbor was big news.

Seated across my bedroom behind me in a sagging wing back chair, Morton Edge sat as usual engrossed in his reading. (I purchased the chair with the payment we received after resolving the Case of The Canary Reciprocity just for his comfort). He reads a book a day. Printed books are a dead art form as far as I'm concerned.

Mirror Image

The Internet is the new library.

I wanted to work from Edge's parent's basement. He insisted we start our PI agency from my bedroom. Truthfully, I was decidedly uncomfortable in my bedroom, especially as I'm not what you would call a *neat* housekeeper. Edge had removed the pile of dirty laundry from the wing chair before he sat down.

"Are there witnesses?" he asked, after I explained about the purported murder of our neighbor, Ivan Silakov, age 35 years who has had no more birthdays in his future. From his accent we deduced Mr. Silakov was a typical Russian immigrant. Our neighborhood watch reported the apparently widowed Mrs. Silakov, nee Mila Bronovitch, was Brooklyn born and raised. Edge and I had never seen or spoken to her, but we were told she was in her early thirties, about ten years older than either of us.

My best friend, Morton Edge, reads three kinds of books: history, and psychology textbooks and, believe it or not, romance novels. He says human motivation is determined by where we come from, and where we are going. He studies our past, our psychological make up, and our capacity for love, he says, to find truth.

I say beans to this idea. To me it's all in the genes.

People are either born good, or they're born bad. Simple.

Don't get the wrong idea. I enjoy a good story as much as the next person, but my tastes lean more to the dark worlds of the graphic novel. Being a Goth I enjoy stories of vampires, wizards, and monsters of every description. The supernatural from the monstrous, to the mythic holds far more interest for me than romance.

My Goth persona is enhanced further by head-to-toe black clothing covering my pale, skinny six-foot frame, and spiked hair dyed oil -black, and white pancake makeup. I've been Goth since I was sixteen, which certainly didn't endear me to my teachers, parents, and law professor, but had come in handy during our investigations when a little intimidation was needed.

Edge calls my obsession with dark side of human nature morbid and unrevealing in his quest for truth.

Edge looked up from his book about the Persian Wars, his almond shaped hazel eyes curious. Whether I agree with his theories about human nature or not, Edge is a genius at deductive reasoning -- even when his deductions reveal the worst about human nature.

Mirror Image

From my computer screen, I read out loud a summary of the information accumulated from our surveillance operations.

Six months ago the Silakov's purchased the house next to my parents on Thomas Street. While our network of informants was unable to provide a detailed workup on the mysterious Russian and his ex-Brooklynite spouse, Edge and I have had Mr. Silakov under observation since the day of their arrival in the neighborhood. Strangely, we have seen nothing of Mrs. Silakov in all that time.

Our network of informants, the neighborhood crew we have dubbed the Newspaper Boy League, had been keeping us informed about the Silakov's movements until the expiry of our six-month surveillance policy. However, there had been no wife sightings in all that time.

Our policy is simple. After six months, when a new neighborhood resident's daily activities become routine and mundane (Edge refers to this as the point of tediousness), we abandon daily surveillance and move to our monthly surveillance and reporting system. Royce, leader of the Newspaper Boy League, provides us monthly surveillance reports. (Kids on bikes delivering papers don't attract much attention.)

The bad news in this situation was that the six-months expired a week ago. The good news was that we came to be aware of the murder of Mr. Silakov, because there was a witness from amongst Royce's network of informants.

Neighborhood busybody, and professional widow, Mrs. Eloise Stein, who resides directly across Thomas Street from my parent's house, witnessed the mysterious Mrs. Silakov shoot her husband from her living room window. While blackouts are troublesome, starlight makes even the darkest night amazingly brilliant and clear.

Unfortunately, when the police arrived on the scene, after phone service was restored and they were able to break away from protecting businesses from potential looters, they did not find a body, at least not a dead one. When they arrived they found a very startled, very much alive Mr. Silakov seated in his living room reading a copy of the Wall Street Journal.

While we don't know what explanation was offered by the Silakovs, we do know the police did not linger at the purported crime scene. From Mrs. Stein's only daughter, Hazy Stein, we know that before departing, the responding homicide detective cautioned the widow Stein against filing false reports in the future, or face severe sanctions.

Mirror Image

Since I am known for being thorough, I naturally relayed all of these details to Edge. With his book open in his lap, his eyes impassive, clear and steady, he listened intently to my every word. I've worked closely with him on many cases so I knew he would apply his considerable analytical skills to weigh each of the details in his mind. He has the ability to filter out only the most pertinent facts of the alleged crime.

After I finished my tale he raised his book to block my view of his narrow, studious features. All I could see of him was the top of his nest of loose brown curls, his pale freckled hands that held the book between us, his forest green sleeveless tee shirt, and his faded blue jeans. On his feet he wore black and white Nikes that he crossed over each other at the ankles.

"Jerome, I wish you to arrange a meeting with Mrs. Stein as soon as possible," he said from behind his book.

"On one condition," I said.

He dropped the book to gaze at me quizzically. "And what might that be?"

"My name is Razor, *not* Jerome if you recall Edge, I asked you to refer to me by my Goth persona more than a year ago." And Edge had been ignoring my request for more than a year.

I hoped that now, with a real case on which to apply our considerable gifts, he might finally acquiesce to my demand.

Edge's eyes crinkled at the corners then flashed with, as I have so oft described in our blog, tolerant amusement. He lowered the book long enough to let me see the brief smile that crossed his pale lips, only to disappear behind his book again. The Persian Empire divided us once again. "If you would then— Razor—"

"Is that an apology?"

His only reply was a snort then silence.

2

We were faced with a dilemma that could be the showstopper.

We were not a registered private investigation firm. Nor will the authorities listen to any evidence we gather unless, as with any citizen, we have solid and substantial facts. Even then we might be charged with inferring with a police investigation.

And how did I know this you ask?

Because today we received a visit from the local constabulary, an NYPD homicide detective named Aimes, who said he was none too pleased with our activities. I was surprised to discover the police actually read my blog entries; though it occurred to me that perhaps someone tipped them off. I also noted that Detective Aimes offered no explanation as to why he continued to have an interest in the Silakovs.

Edge and I have discussed the matter and have decided to continue with our inquiries and share what we learn with the Detective Aimes. It is our fervent hope he may eventually become an ally.

***

Russ Crossley

When I left the house, I was dressed in my favorite black short sleeve shirt—the one with the dark flames design across the front—black cotton pants, thick soled black steel toed boots, and my floor length black leather coat with the red cotton lining. As usual my short hair was gelled for that cool spiky look, and my hair and my goatee were doused with hair oil, to give it that magical sheen. Black eye makeup completed my total Goth look, and I wore my trademark dark sunglasses to hide my eyes.

If my look doesn't intimidate anyone then I must be doing it wrong.

I felt the eyes of the neighbors follow my exaggerated stride as I headed across the street toward the widow's house. I had arranged an appointment with the widow Stein, with the aid of Hazy Stein, who had offered to cover our fee if we proved her mother, had not lost her marble collection. It's rare in this business when you see someone ahs calm about this, as this girl was when she approached me.

As I walked across the burning pavement I felt the blast of the midday sun beating on me from above and below as waves of heat radiated from the blacktop. The oppressive summer heat was moderated slightly by a gentle breeze coming from the south.

Mirror Image

Since this was Saturday the breeze carried with it the smell of fresh cut grass. The air was thick with humidity today consequently my shirt quickly molded itself to my skin.

While I should have left my leather coat behind, I knew I looked far more daunting in it than not, and besides I needed somewhere to bury my trembling hands.

Edge had given me very specific instructions.

I was to interview the widow and her progeny, Hazy, to glean what I could about the murder they may have witnessed in order to determine if they had seen a real murder, or to confirm they had invented the entire affair.

I was also to probe for any other events before or after the day of the alleged murder, which Edge would use to create a timeline. We hoped a timeline would provide us with clues and/or suspects to continue the investigation. Failure was not an option. A lot hung on this interview.

If from this interview we obtained additional clues, we hoped to follow up with other interviews and so on to the ultimate resolution of the case. I like to think of our process as Hansel-and-Gretel-follow-bread-crumbs-in-a-forest-filled-with-monsters-to-find-the-ugly-step-sister.

Russ Crossley

What puzzled me at first was how Mr. Silakov could be alive yet murdered at the same time, until Edge pointed out what should have been obvious. Mr. Silakov must have an identical twin brother who had been somehow substituted for the late Ivan Silakov prior to the murder. The question of why still required a response. But this was the one question we were unable to answer without more facts.

Within our investigative service, my job was to gather facts from the information super-highway, and when necessary, do the legwork and interview witnesses and suspects. I was always nervous about the latter, having interviewed persons who turned out to be suspects in the course of several investigations. I have discovered, sometimes too late, you never know who is the suspect, and who is the witness, until the interviewee answers your questions, flees the scene, or attacks you.

In my experience most suspects don't flee after being cornered. That only happens in the movies.

The last suspect I interviewed, one Eric Fairchild, who confessed to absconding with Sindy Parker's comic books, struck me over the head with a garden gnome when I asked him too many questions he didn't like. The resulting gash required six stitches to close the wound.

The incident also set off a parental earthquake the equivalent of 9.2 on the Richter scale in my otherwise happy home due to the resulting rise in my father's medical insurance premiums.

Those events were still fresh in my mind, and I did not care to see anything similar repeated, as I walked toward Mrs. Stein's residence.

As you'd expect, Edge said the Fairchild incident served as an example of not being adequately prepared. But how do you prepare to be a wackadoodle for the deranged?

Mrs. Stein's house was a split-level bungalow with lime green siding. The front door was steel, painted white and fashioned to look like wood. The front yard was small, no more twenty feet wide and ran no more than that from the sidewalk to the large picture window that faces the street. From the sidewalk I saw a red and white flower patterned sofa against the back wall of the living room.

The pale green grass was pitted with dry brown spots about the size of a silver dollar, as if someone had syringed the weeds. Two narrow flowerbeds of dark brown earth framed the patch of grass. One contained a perfectly straight row of three foot high banana-yellow roses; the other a matching row of ruby-red roses.

The sweet perfume of the roses filled my nostrils as I walked up the stepping stones to a flight of three maroon-colored concrete stairs that ran up to a landing where a straw door mat, in shape of a half circle, that reminded me of a smile, lay in front of the door.

It occurred to me that there wasn't a weed visible in either rose bed. I made a mental note of this and the incongruence of the brown spots in the lawn versus the symmetry of the flowerbeds, and decided to include these details in my report to Edge.

As I came to the door I pressed the doorbell. Immediately, I heard the sound of church bells coming from the other side of the door. This was followed by a small dog barking or, more correctly, shrilly yapping. I rolled my eyes. I was now officially worried about the hem of my expensive leather pants.

After I'd waited for what seemed like an eternity, beads of sour sweat tickling my face, the door opened a crack and a single dark eye peered at me. The door's bronze-colored security chain was visible through the narrow opening.

"Good, it's you." I recognized the Vulcan nerve pinch inducing voice of Hazy behind the cyclopean eye from our earlier conversation.

Mirror Image

The door closed and I heard the rattle of the chain being removed then the door swung open. I was surprised to find a kindred spirit behind the voice. The in-person Hazy Stein was also a Goth.

Oil black hair, weaved into tight corn rolls, a black leather miniskirt, fishnet stockings, knee high leather boots with thick soles that made her as tall as me, a nose ring, cheek and eyebrow piercings, and multiple stud earrings that ran up her delicately shaped ears made Hazy the most beautiful woman I had ever seen. Her dark haunted eyes, surrounded by carbon black makeup, against a whitewashed face, lit up when she welcomed me inside.

"You're Razor of Razor and Edge, right?"

I nodded and told her I was.

"Do I have ta pay ya now?" she asked, as she led me into the living room.

I replied that I would discuss remuneration at the conclusion of the case. It is another of our policies that we never accept a fee for unsolved cases. Our motto is: *No crime solved, you no pay. Satisfaction Guaranteed 24/7.*

I know…it needs work.

A ball of fluff I recognized as one of those miniature breed of terriers, followed closely behind his mistress, occasionally peering up at me.

I don't know what kind of damage this diminutive dog could inflict if I was an axe murderer, but at least my pant hems were safe for the moment.

The sofa I had seen from the sidewalk was only the tip of the weird iceberg. The room looked like a museum dedicated to the worship of the tacky tourist knick-knack.

Glass shelves rested on steel brackets. On the shelves were objects des arts from the twilight zone gift shop.

Bobble heads of every President since Washington were lined up on one set of shelves that ran up one wall from just off the pink shag carpet to just below the white textured ceiling. On another set of shelves were rows of three-inch tall cast bronze statuettes of what looked like twisted versions of birds of prey. Eagles, ravens, and some fantasy creatures such as swallows with teeth, hawks, and some birds I was pretty certain never actually existed. At least not in the real world.

Another set of shelves contained lunch boxes depicting sixties television shows.

Every shelf was more bizarre than the next until I spied a set of shelves containing uncounted picture frames of all shapes and sizes.

Mirror Image

The pictures in the frames were as varied as the frames themselves. There were pictures of elderly men, women of every age and description, children of every ethnicity, and frames with travelogue scenery from Paris to Lake Placid. Given this display of weirdness I somehow suspected none of the people depicted were immediate or even distant relations. I assumed Mrs. Stein collected the frames themselves, not what was in them.

The air reeked of glass polish and the rotten egg stench reminiscent of the silverware cleaner my Mom used every Thanksgiving to polish the family silver. Obviously, the widow Stein kept her treasures well maintained.

Hazy must have seen a bewildered expression like mine before, because she felt she had to explain. With a heavy sigh she sat down on the flowery couch patting the cushion next to hers with the flat of her hand to indicate where I should sit. I sat down. My mouth hung open. My eyes riveted by the strange sights surrounding me. The dog sat at my feet gazing up at me as if he were waiting for something.

What people collect always amazes me. I personally had never collected anything, if you don't count Goth wear, but then that's about fashion and certainly not anything like what Mrs. Stein collected.

"Mom collects…things…ahhh…from…well," from lotsa places actually…garage sales, Goodwill, the Franklin Mint, other collectors…" Her voice dropped in volume. "A lotta junk, don't ya think?"

I wanted to agree with her, but since I was supposed to ingratiate myself to these people, discretion was the preferable tactic.

I shook head slowly and pulled my eyes away from a picture of the Taj Mahal. Not a photograph of the ancient palace, mind you, a yellowing postcard in silver-plated frame. "No. Of course not. I collect stuff myself."

Hazy smirked and crossed arms over her smallish bosom and sank her lean frame into the over-stuffed sofa cushion behind her. "Yeah. Right."

I looked at her. "Sorry, it's just that I've never seen anything like this and--"

She laughed brightly. I felt my face grow warm. "It's okay, Razor, you don't have to explain." Her smile faded and her expression became serious.

"I wanted to meet you and Edge before I hired you." She glanced toward the front door and asked, "Where's your partner?"

I shook my head and said, "Sorry, but Edge never meets the clients outside of our…ummm…office. He says it taints his objectivity.

He prefers to have me gather the facts of the case and then together we analyze the evidence."

"You mean he analyzes the evidence don't you?"

I looked at her with a quizzical eye. A sly grin came over her features. "I've read your blog, and I spoke with Bernie Waters about you and Edge," she said.

***

Bernie Waters had his television remote control stolen by one of his guests at his April Fools party last April 1st. Because Bernie had been driving his family crazy looking for it, his daughter Viola most of all, Edge and I, at Volia's request, had taken the case. At first it seemed impossible to solve until I conducted the initial interviews.

The party guests included six husbands and their wives all about the same age as my parents. The first wall of resistance I met was, understandably, my youth and manner of dress. After all, why would a group of middle class adults cooperate with some Goth kid in a leather coat who looked like Dracula minus the fangs? Excellent question.

Since Bernie Waters was their boss, the door to that issue was pretty much open to me.

Naturally, when I started my inquiries, any possible culprit among this group clammed up tighter than the defensive line of the Chicago Bears. To a man they were understandably fearful of losing their jobs if found guilty of any wrong doing never mind the kidnap of the bosses remote was an April fools prank (and a great one at that, given how us guys are glued to the things). The fear in their eyes told me that the discovery of the guilty party was going to be difficult, if not impossible, even using my usual tells. Evidently their boss didn't share my twisted sense of funny.

The schemey-fingers-twitch and the sweaty-armpit-test work far better than you might think to give away someone who wants to hide the truth.

Collectively this group produced enough perspiration to fill the great lakes twice over, and with all the finger twitching and eye-contact avoidance, they made Simon Legree look like he belonged in a Nunnery. Even after Waters promised he wouldn't fire anyone, there was still no confession. I know I didn't believe him either.

It's like Edge says, never come between a man and his television remote unless you really want to suffer the wrath of a man who can no longer channel surf.

Mirror Image

Finally, after a week of getting nowhere, we managed to root out the perpetrator using one of the oldest tricks in the big book of April Fools pranks. We lied.

Edge suggested it, actually.

I hacked into the phone company records to extract the six suspects home and office phone numbers. I then set up duplicate phone mailboxes on their home phones. I recorded a voice message, using a synthetic voice generator, on each of the six boxes saying we had identified each man as the one who took the remote. In the message I said we were about to turn over the name of the guilty person to Waters, unless he paid us one thousand dollars in small bills. And we made it a condition that he delivered the remote to us personally along with the money.

The next morning, we waited until we were certain they were at the office, then had these ghost boxes (as I dubbed them) call each of the six men simultaneously using another program I developed. A program, by the way, that was, and still is, a work of pure genius.

Edge said the program was adequate for the job – a high compliment from him.

Waters waited with us at the house until the perpetrator showed up.

Too bad it turned out to be his son Maxwell. Apparently, poor old Max wasn't living up to the family name as heir apparent to his father's business empire. He explained he took the remote to punish his father. It was an act of youthful rebellion to draw attention to himself, which it certainly did.

No one was fired, Max and his dad worked out an equitable arrangement and, most importantly, this case made us a legend in the neighborhood.

Naturally, we also had to sign a non-disclosure agreement promising never to speak about the case, so as not to besmirch the Waters name, which meant I couldn't talk about the case on our blog. But word of mouth and unconfirmed rumors, from anonymous sources close to the investigation (fed by yours truly), ground out of the neighborhood gossip mill faster than a flight of F15's could deliver shock and awe to downtown Baghdad.

***

The question in my mind now was how much had Waters told Hazy about his case? I'm sure she'd heard the rumors, and while our blog doesn't contain the details, it does list him as a client under solved cases. We titled his case 'The Case of the Ghostly Boxes'.

Our blog also lists three cases described as unsolved and still under active investigation.

I hadn't added this new Stein case to the list of active, unsolved cases yet because we aren't sure if it qualifies as one, and we haven't given it a name yet.

"How do you know, Mr. Waters?" I asked.

A brief smile curled her lips and her eyes flashed with amusement. "I thought you were the detective?"

I nodded. "Yes. Yes I am, but I haven't yet acquired the ability to read minds. And since the client wishes the details of that case to remain confidential I'm surprised he told you anything."

A frown creased her forehead. She knew she'd been out maneuvered. Besides being smoking hot she was smoking smart. Edge referred to such people as lethal combinations.

Her full lips opened alluringly and she licked them with a stud-pierced tongue. "Truth is, Razor he didn't tell me much of anything. He did say you and Edge had done an excellent job for him. And that I could trust your discretion."

I nodded again. "Yes, he's correct. Clients privacy is respected, especially in such delicate matters." I emphasized the word delicate.

Her thin black eyebrows rose up her pasty forehead. "But what about your blog? You seem to share a lot of information with the world."

I chuckled. "I assure you not everything is shared, Miss Stein."

Her eyes narrowed. She seemed uncertain until I added. "Miss Stein, if you're concerned that the murderer will know who witnessed the act, rest easy in the knowledge that he, or she, will not see your name or your mother's name on our blog if you do not wish it there." I looked into her eyes. "You have my personal guarantee."

Her shoulders visibly relaxed just as Mrs. Eloise Stein came into the room carrying a silver serving tray in her hands. The smell of fresh brewed orange pekoe tea and warm shortbread cookies filled the air. My stomach grumbled. I knew I should have eaten more than that leftover. half-eaten Mars Bar for breakfast.

Mrs. Stein was not a typical widow: tall, willowy, with shoulder length blonde hair, dressed in a watermelon colored mini-skirt, a matching sleeveless shirt with spaghetti straps. Her makeup was tastefully applied. Her eyes were the blue reminiscent of a glass marble.

What little I could see of the swell of her breasts underneath the shirt suggested she didn't require a bra. Her feet were bare and her toenails were painted a light pinkish color.

Mirror Image

According to The Newspaper Boy League, her late husband, who died of cancer five years ago, was CEO of a Fortune 500 company. His will left her with several million dollars worth of stock options.

Though she was over twice my age she was still a very attractive and desirable woman. No wonder Edge refused to meet with clients. These two would be hottie bookends on anyone's bookshelf. The moisture in my mouth evaporated just looking at them.

"Hello," she said, a warm smile on her face. She set the tray on the brass and wood coffee table. I thought the table looked more like a coffin than a piece of furniture.

Without asking she poured three cups of tea and placed two each of chocolate cookies on three white china side plates, one for each of us. She handed a plate to me then she did the same for her daughter and finally placed one in front of her. Mrs. Stein was a real Miss Manners.

"Cream and sugar, or lemon?" she asked before pouring her own cup and taking a seat across from me in an over-stuffed chair that matched the sofa. She sat with the cup held perfectly balanced, resting on her open palm. Her long, bare, very shapely legs she crossed at the ankles.

Her steady, intelligent eyes locked on mine.

"Uuuh…no…thank…you…nothing," I finally managed to stammer. Mrs. Stein was a whirlwind of pent up energy.

"My daughter tells me you and Mr. Edge may be able to help me?" She raised her cup to her full lips and took a sip her dark eyes gazing steadily at me over the rim of her teacup.

I glanced at Hazy who quickly avoided my eyes by dropping her gaze to study the suddenly fascinating contents of her teacup.

Looking back at the widow Stein I cleared my throat before I said, "Yes. Well. From what I understand you are alleging—"

"I am alleging nothing, young man! I saw a man shot to death through my living room window." Her dark eyes seethed with anger.

"I'm not saying I don't believe you, Mrs. Stein, it's just that the police have investigated and have dismissed your claim." Her face went scarlet with pent up rage, and looked about to burst like a child's balloon, until I held up one hand to silence her and continued. "Our view is that you have seen something of significance, maybe even a murder. But, until we investigate the matter further we will not know for certain what we are dealing with."

Mirror Image

I intentionally left out Edge's theory concerning a twin brother. Though I agreed with his deduction, sharing unproven theories this early in an investigation tends to muddy the waters, and may even create unintentional wild turkey shoots.

Mrs. Stein frowned then her eyes narrowed. "Young man…Razor isn't it?" I nodded. "Razor, you certainly dress the part of a Goth." She tilted her head slightly toward Hazy a look of disgust on her face then added, "Believe me, I know Goth. But you seem far too well spoken and certainly don't sound like some of Hazy's other friends. How can that be?"

I knew what she really meant was she doubted my credentials to investigate her case so I explained. "One year at NYU law school, Mrs. Stein. After leaving school we decided to pool our talents and start our own private investigation company. Edge and I are writing our private investigator state examination next month."

"And why would you leave school?" Her tone suggested scoff.

From the corner of my eye I spied Hazy's shocked and angry glare at her mother's words. And she was right. The reasons for my defection from higher education were none of her mother's business, but I really wanted this case and she needed to trust us.

Against my better judgment I decided to explain.
I'm certain Edge would have disagreed with me so
I decided to omit this portion of our encounter from
my report. He didn't need to know I would fall on
my metaphoric sword if necessary for the good of our
joint venture.

"Mrs. Stein, I am not disposed to tell you or
anyone else anything of my personal life-choices
but…" I paused and drew in a deep breath to steady
myself. I smiled inwardly because this gesture caused
the widow Stein's facial expression to soften. "I will
tell you. I was bored with academia and, at the risk
of sounding arrogant, according to the Cattell test
I have an IQ of 168, which, as I'm sure you know,
is considered by some as reasonably intelligent." I
smiled.

I watched Mrs. Stein's shoulders relax until they
slumped forward her hands in her lap worrying them.
Her eyes became watery.

"I'm sorry, Razor it's just…"

"Please go on…" you little mood shifter you.

"It's just that…seeing a man shot to death is a
very unsettling experience."

That was when the water works started.

Mirror Image

She pulled a crumpled piece Kleenex from an invisible pocket in her skirt and used it to dab her cheeks to absorb the tears that flowed from her red-rimmed eyes.

"Yes, Mrs. Stein, I am quite certain it is." If this burst of emotion was to be believed then I was fast becoming a convert to the notion that she just might have indeed witnessed a murder. Time would tell.

As she regained control, I said, "Now, Mrs. Stein why don't you tell me everything…and please start from the beginning. By the beginning I mean I want to know everything you saw that happened across the street up to a week before the murder, and anything you saw that appeared out of the ordinary in the days after the murder. Please be a thorough as possible, no detail is too minor when we're conducting an investigation."

She nodded then a puzzled expression crossed her tear stained face. "Aren't you going to take notes?"

I pointed my left index finger at the side of my head like a pistol. "Photographic memory."

"Oh…" Mrs. Stein looked sheepish.

I looked at Hazy and said, "After I finish here, Hazy, would you accompany me to my house to meet with Edge and me?"

Hazy nodded slowly, her eyes wide, as if she feared her mother and was afraid to say yes without permission. It was odd behavior for an adult woman. Something about this mother daughter relationship was off. I wished I could have determined what was wrong. Hazy certainly didn't appear eager to talk about what was bothering her. Too much fear in those eyes. For now, I let it go.

Her mother wasn't crazy, but she was certainly unusual

3

By the time Mrs. Stein finished her story, I had finished my tea and cookies. I thanked her and placed the cup and plate on the tray on the coffee table. The dog, whose name she said was Rug (I assume the dogs American Kennel Club registered name is Rug Rat, given his diminutive stature), followed me to the front door looking proud that he was escorting me out, his little nose in the air and his tail wagging furiously.

At the front door I apologized to Mrs. Stein for leaving my shoes on with her shag carpet. She dismissed my concern with a wave of her hand explaining the rug had been Scotch guarded. She told me any dirt or water I'd tracked in would be vacuumed up later. She vacuumed her carpets every evening before retiring. With a dog about, the hair would build up if you didn't keep ahead of it.

I thought about telling her terriers didn't shed any more hair than a human being, but decided to remain silent. From my study of her during our interview, I judged Mrs. Stein was in a very fragile emotional state.

If I corrected her about her dog, it would only worsen her already weakened state, and besides it seemed pointless and rather heartless to add to her already evident emotional baggage.

Once we were outside on the sidewalk the warm, humid air bore down on me. Hazy finally asked me the question I so wished to avoid. "So? What do you think? Is my mother crazy?"

I sighed inwardly and said, "No, I don't believe your mother is mentally ill by any legal definition of the word. However, I do think your mother's emotional state is not the best. She's suffered some severe shocks in the past few years, what with your father's sudden death, and now witnessing a murder—"

"So you believe she saw Mr. Silakov murdered by his wife?"

"What I said was she witnessed a murder, I just didn't say the victim was Mr. Silakov, nor did I say Mrs. Silakov killed anyone." From the corner of my eye I saw her look of surprise. I smirked. "All will be revealed when we speak with Edge."

She shrugged her narrow shoulders and emitted a soft grunt apparently satisfied with my explanation.

Mirror Image

Secretly I hoped Edge would be able to unravel this mystery and reveal the chewy center at the heart of the crime.

My parent's house is a Westerleigh rancher with a finished basement, hardwood floors and three bedrooms. Two of the bedrooms have been joined to form my bedroom/office as the base of operations for Razor and Edge investigations. Mom and dad had a contractor knock down a wall between bedroom numbers two and three. I so love being the only child.

Mom and Dad are the associates in a Manhattan law firm consequently they work long hours. We pass each other like ships at sea, only seeing each other from our respective crows nests. Though this was Saturday, they were involved in a complex corporate litigation for the past several weeks, so they'd be in the city for most of the day.

When Hazy and I entered we found Edge sitting in the kitchen at the table eating a bowl of cereal, his nose buried in a book.

He glanced up from his book. The sliding glass door leading to the backyard in the family room off the kitchen was open. What little breeze there was did nothing to moderate the temperature in the room.

Edge was dressed in his usual uniform of blue jeans, Nikes, and pale green tee shirt. No one knew how many green tee shirts he owned.

His eyes went back to his book as we sat down across from him. He shoveled another heaping tablespoon of cereal into his mouth. It crunched loudly. The open box of Energy Bombs sat in the middle of the breakfast table in front of him. In this case 'energy' is a code word for 'loaded to max with sugar'.

"Breakfast of champions?" I asked.

Edge looked at me with an annoyed expression on his narrow features. He pushed his cereal bowl away after he closed his book. His attention shifted to Hazy who sat in the chair across the table from him, her arms resting on the table her eyes apprehensive. "Miss Stein I gather?" he asked. She nodded uneasily, her eyes avoiding his studious gaze.

Edge shifted his attention to me. "How did the interview go?"

I described La Casa de Stein, its contents, the appearance of Mrs. Stein, and my doubts about her emotional state.

Edge sat silently listening until my catalog was complete, then he said, "And the day of the murder?"

Mirror Image

It was time for the meat between the two halves of the bun. "Eloise Stein says on the night of the blackout, as she was sitting in the dark in her living room star-gazing, she spotted a sudden flash of light in the Silakov's living room window across the street. Curiosity getting the best of her she made her way across the street—"

"What time was this?" interrupted Edge.

"About midnight—"

"Mom likes to stay u—" said Hazy.

Edge silenced her with a look then nodded to me to continue.

"Mrs. Stein says she crept up to the front window of the Silakov's house. Inside she says she saw Mr. Silakov on his side on living room floor. His head was a bloody mess."

"How is she certain it was Mrs. Silakov that shot him—-if indeed he was shot at all?"

"Mrs. Stein says while she was watching, Mrs. Silakov entered the room carrying a pistol with a silencer affixed to the barrel."

Edge looked thoughtful as he mulled over these facts then asked, "What did she do then?"

"She went home and waited for the phone lines to clear, then called the police." Edge nodded.

I added, "Due to the blackout, the phone lines were not available until six in the morning. Even then the police were unable to respond for several hours after that."

"Did Mrs. Stein witness any subsequent unusual activity at the Silakov's residence while she waited for the police?"

"No. Nothing."

"And in the days preceding the murder?"

"The Silakov's were doing some remodeling on their kitchen so there were rolls of heavy plastic left by the contractors lying about. She also witnessed courier delivery vans coming and going from the Silakov's house at least twice per week since they moved into the neighborhood."

"Anything else?"

"No."

Edge looked to Hazy. "Do you have something to add, Miss Stein?"

"My mom's not crazy?"

A trace of amusement flashed across Edge's hazel eyes. "No, Miss Stein I agree. Your mother is certainly not 'crazy'. I do have a couple of questions for you, though. Where were you and the dog during the events described by—" Edge hesitated, "--by Razor?"

Mirror Image

"How do you know about the dog? I never said anything about a dog," I said. It was at times like this, when Edge's power of deduction was at full strength, he's like a finely tuned instrument.

His steady gaze fell on me. "I detected the scent of *canis lupus famliaris* the moment you both entered this room. And since neither you nor I own such an animal, and since the scent is stronger on Miss Stein than yourself, I deduced she spends considerably more time around such an animal than you." His brow creased in thought as he shifted his gaze to Hazy again. "I also deduced that you do not live with your mother on a full time basis."

Hazy looked surprised. "How do you know that?"

"Razor said Mrs. Stein was alone during the blackout. This suggests you and the dog were not at home, or she would certainly have asked you to accompany her across the street. Alternately, she would have woken you and confided in you her fears upon returning from her covert surveillance. Since you insist your mother isn't 'crazy' I take this to mean you were not present, and therefore did not witness the events described by your mother."

Hazy's eyes narrowed. "And Rug?"

Edge smiled. "The dog's name, I gather, is Rug?" She nodded.

He snorted. "Rather simple really. If the dog had been present, it would have been with her, and would very likely have barked to alert the killer, or killers, to your mother's presence. Since your mother is very much alive I deduce the dog was also absent on the day of the murder."

A look of amazement washed over Hazy's features and her mouth formed an O shape. "Uhhh… Rug was with me at my apartment that night. The dog groomer mother prefers is down the street from my place. So I took him home with me so I could take him for his hair cut the next morning." Her gaze shifted to me. "He's amazing," she breathed.

"I sometimes loan him out for parties, weddings, and bar mitzvahs…" I felt Edge's glare on me. "Seriously though, what did the police say?"

Hazy's eyes suddenly went wide and her face drained of what minimal color there was. "You think Mrs. Silakov would have killed my mother too?"

Edge ignored Hazy's shock at learning of her mother's brush with death and instead shrugged his shoulders. "Whoever murdered Mr. Silakov was able to convince the authorities that he or she did not murder anyone, therefore I suspect whoever is responsible would also have no qualms about murdering any witnesses."

"Is my mother still in danger?"

Edge shrugged again. "No, I don't think so."

"How do you know?"

Before my friend could respond, I decided to jump into the conversation. "Since the police appear to have rejected your mother's claims I…" I smiled at Edge who nodded, "we expect the perpetrator anticipated someone would see the crime and had planned for just such a contingency." Hazy looked puzzled. "You see we think Mr. Silakov's twin brother was substituted for the murdered Mr. Silakov."

Now Hazy looked uncertain. "And you can prove this?"

I smirked and shook my head. "Not yet. But we will."

4

Hazy left for her mother's house after she explained that the police had said nothing, other than that they found Mr. Silakov very much alive when they visited the Silakov residence. In fact, they told Mrs. Stein that Mr. Silakov was shocked that they would think he was murdered. They told him they had a witness but that he had maintained his ignorance.

Edge sat in his chair, his brow furrowed in thought. He processed the facts of the case for an hour before he spoke. While I waited, I conducted Internet research and sent out an e-mail to my contact at the Department of Homeland Security asking about Mr. Silakov's immigration status. Some of our NYU classmates now worked at DHS and they were always willing to aid in our investigations if they led to illegal or suspicious individuals. We were listed with DHS as confidential informants, which gave us access. Careers are often made on the backs of others.

Finally Edge grunted and stood. "Let's make some coffee," he said.

We were seated at the kitchen table while the coffee pot gurgled as filtered coffee streamed into the glass carafe beneath the drip basket to fill the room with the smell of fresh brewed coffee.

Edge finally spoke.

"We do not have sufficient facts to draw any definitive conclusions," he said. I frowned and shifted in my chair. Edge waved one hand at me. "I did not say we couldn't speculate—"

The silver phone hung on a cradle affixed to the wall rang loudly, interrupting him. I stood and plucked it off the cradle. It was a cordless model so I was able to bring it back to the table and sat down before pressing the talk button.

"Hello?"

I glanced at Edge.

"Hello, Hazy." A look of impatience crossed Edge's features. I knew he was eager to share his theory with me.

"Yes, Hazy. What can I do for you?"

"Uuhh…there is one thing I didn't share with you…" Her voice trailed off and I detected fear in her tone.

"Go on."

"Well, you see last night I saw a murder but I was afraid you might think I'm crazy…"

Given who her mother was I was tempted to agree with her diagnosis. Frankly, I was quickly developing serious concerns about both of them, but I held my tongue.

Russ Crossley

"I saw Mr. Silakov murder Mrs. Silakov."

5

A dead man murdered his wife who the day before murdered him. If there was ever a puzzle that needed to be unraveled it was this one.

In the years I have known him I have never seen Edge so agitated. I hung up the phone and when I told Edge what Hazy had just told me, he was like a child on Christmas Eve. He leapt from his chair and began to pace the kitchen.

"Coffee?" I asked. I watched Edge pace back and forth. It was like sitting at center court at the U.S. Open Tennis Tournament.

He shook his head. "Have Royce here in 30 minutes. And send another e-mail to our DHS friends. We need to know more about Mr. and Mrs. Silakov's siblings. We require home and work addresses, phone numbers, dates of birth and, if we can get them, physical descriptions focusing on distinguishing marks etcetera. Also, I need to know what's in those courier envelopes."

I poured myself a cup of coffee then, after telephoning Royce's cell phone and he agreed to be at my house in twenty-five minutes.

While we waited I went to my bedroom and e-mailed my DHS contact to request the information about the Silakov's and their siblings.

I came back fifteen minutes later with a copy of the e-mail response to my first inquiry. In nineteen ninety-eight, when she was still Mila Bronovitch, Mrs. Silakov sponsored Mr. Silakov's immigration to the United States. He received his green card only last year.

Miss Bronovitch's application listed her as Mr. Silakov's fiancée. I've heard tell that to maintain a long distance relationship can sometimes be murder. In the Silakov's case it turned out to be the other way around.

Edge merely grunted, he had finally ceased pacing and was now seated at the table with a cup of steaming black coffee in front of him. He read the copy of the message I had handed him.

I sipped my coffee in silence, respecting Edge's concentration. I enjoy watching the keen mind behind those brooding eyes analyze, strain, and weigh every fact for the minutest connectivity. Hazy's addition of a second murder had forced him to reevaluate his earlier theory.

The doorbell sounded in the front hall. I stood and left the kitchen to let Royce in.

Mirror Image

Royce is lean and muscular for his sixteen years. Today he was wearing white runners, low rise sport socks, a pair of sea green shorts and a white tee-shirt with green piping along the outside of sleeves. His Mets baseball cap was on backwards, designed to cover his blonde crew cut. I have never understood why anyone would wear a baseball cap backwards when it's designed to shade the eyes. Good thing I'm not competing to be the next top model.

Once we were seated at the table and Royce had a glass of fizzy cola that I had poured, in front of him, Edge laid out, in chronological order, the events, as we knew them. Royce listened intently to us talk about the case. For a kid of sixteen he had remarkable concentration. It was likely this ability that led Edge to recruit him to head up The Newspaper Boy League.

Royce had a team of two boys and a girl working for him, ranging in age from 12 to 14, with the girl in the middle. He paid better than a paper route, so Royce had his pick of neighborhood kids from which to recruit. Bicycle riding skills were high on his list of job requirements.

Royce had a notebook out and was taking notes as Edge spoke.

Edge ended by asking a question, "Royce, in addition to what we already know do have you anything else that would be useful?"

Royce shook his head. "These are the last people I would have thought of as murderers."

"Why?" I said.

Royce looked surprised. "You don't know? Mrs. Silakov lives in a wheelchair. That's why they're re-modeling their kitchen."

I looked at Edge. The sinking feeling in the pit of stomach meant I knew what he was going to say. But I had to state the obvious. "I'm sorry, Royce but even a small child can use a gun—"

Royce lips formed a sly smile. "Not if you're a quadriplegic you can't."

***

Royce's words went over like a lead balloon. I was the first to burst the bubble of silence that followed. "We really need more information. Somehow we've been in the dark since the beginning."

"There was a blackout ya know," said Royce sarcastically.

Mirror Image

Ignoring Royce's attempt at humor Edge looked thoughtful then said, "There are four possibilities: the widow and her daughter lied, an unlikely possibility because I can not think of a motive for them to lie. The widow and her daughter are equal parts insane and delusional, again I find this unlikely as I do not recall insanity as being a genetic trait, they witnessed a heavenly miracle and a wheelchair bound quadriplegic shot someone with a handgun she could not hold, or Mrs. Stein and Hazy witnessed a devious plot manufactured for their benefit."

"Until we have proof in the form of a body, or some other physical evidence, I cannot say for sure which of these possibilities is the answer."

I gaped at Edge. I'd never seen him this uncertain. "You really think they witnessed a miracle?"

A mischievous smile crossed Edge's face. "I think that's the least likely possibility as we have two murders and lightning rarely strikes twice. More importantly I somehow don't think God would heal someone in order that they could perpetrate a murder. However, as the poet once said, all things are possible on heaven and earth so I am forced to consider this possibility."

Before I could react, Edge turned his attention to Royce who watched our exchange with a sardonic expression on his face. No doubt he was proud to have one-upped the great Morton Edge. "Royce, I must ask you to do something that might be considered illegal. This action falls in the category of the greater good therefore the normal rule of law does not apply, however, if you wish to decline I will understand." He paused to let his words sink in. "I need you to intercept one of the courier envelopes before it's delivered to the Silakov residence and bring it to me."

"Do you want me to open it?" asked Royce.

"No. I will assume that responsibility."

Royce nodded his chair scraped across the kitchen linoleum as he stood and was gone before the echo of the front door slamming came from the hallway.

I leaned forward and looked into Edge's eyes. "What do you really think?" I asked.

He regarded me calmly his eyes still as a mid-summer pond. "We are embarking on a dangerous path from which we may not return."

I felt a shiver run down my spine.

6

Edge dispatched me for some covert surveillance of the Silakov property. Shortly after midnight I left for their house, my mission clearly defined: find something we can use.

With a flashlight in hand, the batteries were nearly exhausted so the device did little more than cast a soft glow, I made my way to the rear of the property. Because I am not the most athletic person on Staten Island, if a ravenous canine had been on the other side of that fence, the dog would have converted to a raw human food diet fairly easily.

I arrived at the rear of the house where I saw piles of discarded debris from the kitchen renovation as reported by Royce and his crew. Shattered kitchen cabinetry, wall board, a stainless steel sink, and cracked pale green cove top counters stacked askew one atop the other rose in piles like monuments to '70's tacky.

Just as Royce had described, there were large rolls of heavy plastic scattered about the trampled grass. The plastic was used to make temporary walls during the renovation to keep dust from spreading between rooms inside the house.

It was odd, but the work seemed to have stopped, because there were no tools or fresh sawn lumber in sight, and there were no fresh boot prints in the soft grass, which had grown several inches high around the debris piles.

While the blackout could certainly have disrupted the workmen's schedule, I knew this anomaly was something else to add our growing grocery list of clues. Having your kitchen torn up for an extended period was an inconvenience few people would wish to prolong.

I moved around the piles in the dim light—my flashlight offered little in the way of illumination—then stumbled through a mound in the grass at the rear of the piles of debris. I directed the weak beam downward and squinted at the freshly dug soil. There was a man-made mound in the earth that had very nearly caused me to fall on my face. I sank onto my haunches as I picked up a handful of the loose soil. The soil was dark, dry to the touch, and had an earthy smell that reminded me of spring.

I froze when it dawned on me this soil had been turned some time in the last few days.

**

I returned to my bedroom using the back door, so as not to disturb my sleeping parents.

Mirror Image

I found Edge still seated in the wing chair engrossed in a Jennifer Crusie romance novel. He looked up at me as I entered.

"Night gardening?" he said seeing the dark spots on the knees of my black jeans where I had knelt in the dirt. I had tried to dig some of the soil away with my bare hands until I realized if there were anything buried here it would be deeper than I could reasonably dig without a shovel.

I smirked. "You still here?"

He closed his book and placed it in his lap. He wasted no more time on our usual banter when he inquired about my night foray. "New evidence?"

I nodded as I sat down on the edge of my grey and white bed spread. I summarized my observations and ended with my aborted attempt at a large scale excavation operation.

He nodded and stood. "Call me at noon tomorrow. I expect Royce will have our courier package by then. And I will have made some calls." He eyed me knowingly. "Has DHS responded?"

"No, not yet. Hopefully tomorrow."

Edge nodded. "Good. Then we will have the pieces of this puzzle and justice will be served."

I looked at him feeling perplexed. "You know how and why?"

His pale brow creased. "Not just yet, but I have narrowed down the parameters somewhat."

After he was gone I stripped off my soiled clothes and, dressed only in my boxers and my socks, I fell into bed. I was exhausted. It had been a long day but I didn't fall asleep immediately. I sifted through the facts of the case for another hour before I finally drifted off.

***

A printout of the latest e-mail I received from my DHS contact rested on the table next to my bowl of breakfast cereal as I sat bleary eyed at the kitchen table trying to read the back of the box of Sugar Chips cereal. The coffee maker bubbled in the background. I really needed my caffeine fix today.

Edge had eaten the full box of Energy Bombs yesterday so I would have to satisfy my hunger with my least favorite brand of cereal. Since all Edge ever ate was cereal I wasn't surprised. The magical properties of high sugar cereal combined with the caffeine guaranteed you a high for the whole day. I had the sinking feeling this was going to be long and stressful day so if anyone needed a pick-me-up it was me. I could always sleep when I was dead.

I heard the front door slam and Royce saying hello to Edge who didn't reply.

Mirror Image

Morton Edge is a nodder and a head-shaker not a talker.

They appeared in the kitchen and joined me at the table. I had left the plastic jug of milk and had set two empty bowls with two spoons on the table, anticipating they would join me in my a.m. repast.

"Rough night?" asked Royce, taking one of the bowls and filling it to the rim with cereal.

I nodded and looked to Edge who sat slumped in his chair his arms crossed over his chest his expression grim. His hazel eyes were cast down at the table. "What's wrong?" I asked.

"I made a few calls this morning and discovered the contractor hired by the Silakov's was let go a month before the alleged murders."

Alleged? "And?" I asked.

"And that does not fit my timeline," he said, clearly frustrated. This case had really gotten under his skin.

"Well, the good news is I have a reply from DHS." I shoved the two-page e-mail at him. "It appears you were correct. If you look at the dates of birth listed for him and his brother Petra, on page two, you'll see they have the same DOB. Just as you suspected, this confirms they're twins."

Edge reached across the table and picked up the loose pages. His hazel eyes scanned the two pages quickly, then he sat back in his chair and sighed heavily.

I rolled my eyes. "Now what's wrong?"

"This information is incomplete." Edge shook his head. He looked from me to Royce and back again then said, "I suspect Mrs. Silakov also has a twin sister."

7

I considered the ramification of this latest tidbit.
I concluded Edge was right. A twin sister would
certainly explain how a quadriplegic could shoot
someone. A healthy twin sister could sit in the chair,
pretending to be her crippled sister then, when the
intended victim was at his most vulnerable, shoot him
dead. But double fratricide by twin siblings no less?
It was almost too fantastic. If we knew the motive,
we might be able to work backward to our most likely
suspects.

Of course, this still didn't dismiss Mr. Silakov as
the murderer of his wife…except Mr. Silakov was
murdered by his wheelchair bound wife before he
murdered her. My head was spinning just thinking
about this bizarre web we'd weaved.

I quickly went upstairs and fired off another
e-mail to my contact to request additional information
about Mrs. Silakov and her siblings. I gave him
her maiden name as well. I knew DHS's massive
database would include every scrap of information
they had on Mila Bronovitch.

Since we'd been at the table, Royce had finished
one bowl of cereal and had helped himself to another.

He had the pouch he carried that looked like a newspaper delivery boy's newspaper bag still slung around his upper torso. After I had gotten up and poured two cups of coffee for Edge and come back to sit down, Royce reached into his pouch to retrieve the courier pack Edge had asked him to intercept. He slapped the envelope in the middle of the table then shoveled another spoonful of the sugar infused cereal into his mouth.

His azure eyes flitted between us as he crunched the cereal in his mouth. I knew better than to ask him where he had acquired the envelope. And I knew Edge never would since he didn't particularly care.

Edge reached for the envelope. Before opening it, he studied the mailing labels. He held the package with the zipper-like tear away at the top and pulled the tab to open it. The envelope was the size and shape consistent the type used to courier small quantities of documents.

As I suspected there were only two pieces of paper inside. One looked like a transmittal slip the other an invoice.

"Let me guess. That's a receipt for Ginsu knives?" I said.

Edge snorted and held up a document that had the Bank of America logo in the top left corner.

"The Silakov's have an offshore bank account."

Now things were getting interesting. It was like some B movie the plot that was thickening faster than if we'd added roux to the soup. Of course, this wasn't a movie. Real people could be dead. Maybe. I really detest uncertainty.

"What do we do next?"

Edge placed the receipt on the table and frowned. "We don't have much time before they miss this document. I suspect this is the final installment before they depart for greener and very likely more tropical pastures." He picked up the receipt and handed to me.

I looked at the dollar figure of the transfer and was shocked to see the amount. I goggled at it. I had never seen a number with six zeros and a three before it and a dollar sign in front of that. I felt butterflies in the pit of my stomach take off and try to fly through my lower intestines. If the Silakov's didn't receive this document soon, they were going to freak out. I know I would. And if they found out we had it well, I didn't even want to think about what they'd do to us.

The Bank of America Trust and Banking Corporation in the Cayman Islands was where the three million dollars had been deposited. The transfer was authorized by the Mr. Silakov yesterday.

For a dead man he obviously knew how to manage his money.

"We need to find the body," said Edge.

"Living or dead?" said Royce, a sardonic expression on his face.

"You talk as if there is only one body; I thought there were two murders?" I said giving Royce a disparaging look. He grinned and shrugged his narrow shoulders.

Edge looked at me and I knew immediately he had a working theory. He began to lay it out. "I'm beginning to doubt there have been two murders." He eased back in his chair and shook his head. "What we're dealing with here is murder for money. If that receipt is any indication, a lot of money. Someone diverted attention from the real murder using the widow Stein as a witness, someone the police already view as unreliable. If they had a report of a second murder at the same location they would hesitate to respond. Probably not for long, but long enough to allow the Silakov's to leave the country, collect their money, and disappear." He paused and steepled his fingers his elbows on his thighs.

"And whoever is behind the real murder has thus far succeeded at every step of their plan."

Mirror Image

The coffeemaker growled in the silence as it filled the carafe. I wasn't interested in it anymore. The coffee just wouldn't taste the same until this murder was in the solved column.

The air was thick with the pall of depression that had fallen over our little band. The bad guys were winning the war. All we needed was one check mark in the win box. It would go a long way to breaking this case wide open.

"Have you received the names and addresses of Mr. or Mrs. Silakov's siblings from our contact?" said Edge.

I'd forgotten about the e-mail to DHS. "I'll be right back." I went up to my bedroom and checked my e-mail. Sure enough my contact had sent me a list of three names: a sister named Celia, who was five years older than Mila, who lived in Houston Texas, a brother named Robert who lived in Paris France, and a sister who lived in Queens. Her parents were deceased.

The sister who lived in Queens, Helen, was three years older than Mila Silakov so she wasn't a twin. This case was a head scratcher if there ever was one.

How had they faked a woman who lived her wheelchair without a twin sister to substitute for—I stopped in mid-thought.

A light bulb went off in my head. Wait a minute—what if?

I grasped the print of the e-mail in my left hand as I leapt three stairs at a time as I ran down stairs. I burst into the kitchen to find Edge and Royce still seated at the kitchen table. I was breathing hard and took a minute to gather in a breath. "I've got it…" I dragged air into my lungs, "There isn't a twin sister… someone else was sitting in the wheel chair pretending to be Mila Silakov…when Mr. Silakov was shot."

Edge regarded me his eyes warm and yet serious. "It took you long enough," he said. Royce smirked. I shot him a look and his eyes dropped to his cereal bowl.

I shrugged. "There are a lot of stairs."

Edge snorted.

***

I wasn't sure Edge had come to the same conclusion I had between the time I checked the e-mail and came back to the kitchen. I suspect he had already concluded that if Mrs. Silakov didn't have a twin sibling, then someone else had done the dirty deed, if there had been a dirty deed at all. After all, according to the police Mr. Silakov was very much alive.

Mirror Image

There was one more loose end to tie up said Edge and then he would have the complete picture. After that he would call Detective Aimes personally and have him meet us at the Silakov's residence where he would unveil the plot and the perpetrator or perpetrators of the crime or crimes.

I only hoped we did this soon, because my gut instinct was telling me the Silakov's were not long for the Big Apple.

***

I arrived at Helen Carp's (nee Bronovitch) house just after one o'clock in the afternoon. The train and subway were surprisingly crowded for a Sunday afternoon.

Standing in the warm air on the front cement step I felt tickles of perspiration run down my back beneath my Mega Death tee shirt. This time I'd made the correct choice to leave my leather coat in the hall closet. Sometimes you had to sacrifice intimidation for the right not to be a puddle of overheated sweat on someone's doorstep.

The neighborhood was typical for Queens, rows of blue-collar houses with neatly trimmed lawns.

Kids on bikes raced up and down the cracked sidewalks and filled the air with screams of delight and laughter.

In contrast to her neighbors, the postage stamp-sized lawn than ran up to the front steps Helen Carp's single story bungalow was a pale green shaggy carpet dotted with yellow dandelions. To the right of the front steps was a flowerbed that had seen better days. It was filled with yellow straw, withered remnants of shrubs, and two dead sticks that were the only evidence of what had once been a rosebush.

The air smelled smoky and was thick with humidity.

The weathered front door creaked open and a rail thin woman greeted me dressed in gray sweat pants and a man's sleeveless white undershirt. Her feet were bare the toe nails were long, ragged and yellow. Evidently they hadn't been trimmed in a while. Her short black hair was shot through with grey streaks. A cloud of smoke enveloped me and she reeked of the lit cigarette that dangled from her thin lips. Her piggy eyes squinted at me. "Yea?" she said her voice raspy, and not the sexy kind of Demi Moore-like raspy that every young boy dreams about. She looked far older than you'd expect given her age. She had lived a hard life.

Mirror Image

I had to force my eyes to my black New Balance runners and away from her sagging breasts visible beneath the tee shirt. No bra. Great.

"Hi. My name's Jerome Saperstein—"

"I was 'xpectin' some guy name 'o Razor. A guy name 'o Edge call me. You 'im?" She looked at me apprehensively.

"Huh…yes…ma'am…my professional name's Razor—"

She grunted apparently satisfied about my identity and stepped back from the door to admit me. Edge must have described my appearance, which gave some trepidation about what else he'd shared about me with this woman. "Com'on in. I dun't wanta be coolin' off da whole neighborhood."

I stepped inside and she slammed the door behind me. I looked around and saw that unlike the yard, the kitchen was clean, bright, and cheery. There was even a smiley cat faced clock next to a calendar stuck to the wall with a red tipped push pin depicting a scene of a Norman Rockwell-esque New England village. The air smelled of freshly brewed green tea and stale cigarettes. I concluded Mrs. Carp was one of those smoking health nuts.

A round table covered with a plasticized tablecloth dotted with red, yellow, and blue flowers sat in the middle of the room. In the center of the table sat a blue and red tea cozy covered teapot. Given the shape underneath the cozy I assumed it was a teapot.

I heard a soft mew and felt something brush against my right leg. Looking down I saw an orange and white tabby.

"Dun' mind Puck," said Helen Carp, moving to the table wheezing as she sat down heavily in an armless faux oak chair. She coughed from the side of her mouth then took out her cigarette and placed it carefully in a clear glass ashtray heaped with spent butts sitting next to her cup. A half empty bottle of bourbon sat on the table between us. I sat across from her, a matching teacup sitting in front of me.

"Good thing ya came taday," she said matter-of-factly.

I looked at her quizzically. "Cleaning lady jus' left," she said. At first I thought she was joking but her bored expression said just-the-facts—ma'am. Joe Friday would be proud of her.

"Tea?" she offered.

I nodded and she removed the tea cozy then filled both cups in turn. "Cream or sugar?"

I shook my head. She shrugged lifted the bottle of bourbon, splashed some in then raised her cup to her lips and took a loud slurpy sip.

"Did Edge tell you why I wanted to speak with you?" I asked.

"Nope."

Talkative woman. A real chatterbox. "Do you know your brother-in-law, Ivan Silakov, very well?"

Helen Carp snorted. "Dat bum," she scoffed and shook her head in disgust. "He dun't talk ta me no more."

"Why not?"

Her eyes blazed with anger. Good thing I'm not the spontaneous combustible type. " 'Cause 'o my sister, that's why."

"You mean Mila Bronovitch?"

She nodded and retrieved her cigarette from the ashtray, lifting it to her lips she took in a deep drag. After she titled her head back, she blew smoke at the ceiling. I guess she thought if she blew the acrid smoke over my head it wouldn't bother me as much. She was wrong.

I coughed to clear my throat then said, "I understand your sister has a little money to invest?"

Helen Carp's eyes narrowed and she crossed her arms and legs as she studied me.

64

"Why? You want her to invest in sumthin'?"

I shook my head. "No. I'm investigating a murder—"

She looked shocked. "What?! Whose?"

"Well, it's kind of strange…" I decided to shift gears. My sixth sense screamed time was about to run out. My eyes flitted to the cat-faced clock then back at Helen. It was four in the afternoon on Sunday. By Monday morning, once the courier envelope that Royce had intercepted came into their possession, the Silakov's would be headed for JFK and be gone. Adios any chance at justice.

"Is my sister ok?" Helen edged forward on her chair and her trembling hands flat on the table. Her eyes were watery and pleading. Evidently she cared deeply for her sister.

"I'm really not sure—"

"Wot do ya mean yor not sure?" Her face twisted with anger and her pale complexion was reddening with each passing second. Her emotions were running marathon. I needed to clarify the situation for her.

I winced. "I'm sorry, I know I sound confusing, it's just that…" I omitted the names of our witnesses, to protect the innocent.

Instead, I told her about the two pseudo murders of her brother-in-law and her sister, and as Edge had instructed me, I told her about the offshore accounts in the Cayman's.

She hung on my every word, her frown deepened as I explained the details of what we knew or suspected. When I finally finished she eased back in her chair and smoked a newly lit cigarette lit with the glowing stub of its predecessor.

"So you and this Edge fella thinks my sista was murdered for money?" she said. I nodded my head. In response she snorted again. "Youse guys got it all wrong."

"And why would that be, Mrs. Carp?"

"Our father left us shares in a chain of gas stations that ran down the eastern sea board. Between us we have the controllin' interest. Ever heard 'o Gas Hogs?"

I nodded slowly. Who hadn't? The Wall Street Journal reported independents like Gas Hogs were giving the big oil companies migraines with their constant price wars in local markets.

"Could your sister have sold her shares of the company without you knowing?"

The haughty look on her face disappeared, replaced by naked fear as her cheeks drained of color. "She wouldn't do that…" Her voice was a whisper and her eyes shifted signaling me she was uncertain.

"Is there someone you can call?" I asked. I felt all Joe Friday-like inside, and I loved it. The PI business had provided me the opportunity to use the great lines of the crime stories I'd always loved.

She frowned. "Not until tomorrow…maybe I'll call my sister…"

"How about now?" I suggested with a small smile on my lips.

"Yea…good idea." She disappeared into an adjoining room and came back with a portable telephone shaped like the famous Mouse who funded theme parks. She tapped in a telephone number into the keypad set in the rodent's belly. The keys beeped in the silence. I sipped my now cold tea and watched as she listened intently the phone pressed to her right ear. Her face was flushed.

Seated across the table from her I heard a muffled click and a male voice say hello at the other end. At least I assumed it was hello because whatever the man said wasn't said in English.

"Is Mila there?" Her tone suggested a new ice age had set in.

Mirror Image

The barely audible voice switched to English and said something I couldn't make out, but as he spoke Helen Carp's ears grew redder and her cheeks glowed with an inner heat. Finally, she said, "Ok. I'll call back later," then brought the phone down to the table and pressed the end button.

Her watery gaze fell over me. "Somethin's happened…I know somethin's happened." She buried her face in her hands and wept harder than anyone I've ever seen. Her body-wracking sobs shook the table.

"Mrs. Carp, I know this is upsetting but how do you know something's happened to your sister?"

Between choking sobs she said, "Dat…man isn't my brother-in-law…I'd know dat slime weasel's voice anywher—" Unable to hold back her grief any longer she collapsed face down onto her arms and began to weep uncontrollably.

She didn't need to tell me any more. I knew that whoever was at that house across Pinewood Street from mine had sold the gas station shares and was now very rich and about to be very gone. As Edge so often says, follow the money and you'll often find the dark side of human nature.

But this one time, please, couldn't he be wrong?

8

I arrived home just before five to find Edge had a visitor. Or should I say visitors.

At the front door I saw two pairs of black Oxfords sitting on the brown straw mat next to the door. I rolled my eyes. Whoever was here must have been instructed to remove their shoes before entering the front room. We never asked anyone to remove their shoes because the rug came with the house when my parents bought it in 1982. It just didn't matter if anyone wore their shoes in the house. Edge must have been enjoying himself in my absence.

Sure enough, upon entering the front room I found Detective Aimes and another man, I assumed was also a police detective, seated on the saggy tan colored sofa each with a glass of water in front of him on the faux oak coffee table. Aimes was dressed in tan Dockers and a forest green golf shirt. He looked like he'd just walked off the eighteenth green. In contrast, his partner was dressed in the ill-fitted navy Wal-Mart suit that was issued to every police detective, or so it seemed.

They must have been waiting for a while because upon seeing me Detective Aimes said, "It's about time."

I cast Edge a disparaging look. He nodded, a mischievous smile on his lips and a twinkle in his eye.

"Detectives," I said formally, before I sat in the over-stuffed chair that matched the one Edge was seated in.

"Finally," said Aimes, "we can get down to what all this is about."

Aimes's silent partner was a bull of man with a thick neck and a crew cut that made him look like he was an army sergeant about to lead his squad of leathernecks into battle at any moment. His coffee-colored eyes were watchful and I knew the notebook in his massive hands would record every word, every nuance of our discussion. His face was tanned and his arms bulged from the bodybuilder muscles hidden underneath his cheap suit.

"What did Mrs. Silakov's sister reveal?" asked Edge casually.

Aimes looked to me, his expression none too friendly. I wondered if he was about to arrest me for interfering with an official investigation until I recalled Aimes had insisted there was no crime.

I launched into my report. "Apparently, some years ago Mrs. Carp and her sister Mila inherited a small fortune in stock in a small gas station company.

Mrs. Carp was apparently unaware that her sister recently sold all of her Gas Hogs shares and planned to leave the country with the proceeds—"

"How do you know Mila Silakov is going to leave the country? And more importantly how do you know about her sale of stock?" Aimes asked his eyes now slitted in suspicion. His tone suggested he also knew these factoids.

I felt a cold sweat beneath my shirt. Edge sat with a small smile on his narrow features as if nothing in the world was wrong.

Before I could respond Edge said, "Because we have a copy of a sale of shares by Mrs. Silakov and a transfer record from a bank here in New York to an offshore account in the Cayman islands."

Aimes's eyes went wide and his tanned face paled slightly. Even his partner slid forward on the sofa cushion his eyes fierce. "Do you have these documents?" said Aimes.

Edge shook his head. "No. They will be delivered tomorrow morning to the Silakov's residence after which I expect a taxi will appear and the Silakov's will depart for the airport."

"So what do you want us to do about all this?" said Aimes. "At this point we don't have enough evidence to apply for a warrant.

"What we have is an unreliable witness who says she witnessed a murder we confirmed did not happen. And we have some documents that we cannot see that show the Silakov's have money in an offshore account. Which is not a crime, by the way."

Aimes eyes opened disingenuously. "Ya know I checked you two out and according to some of your neighbors. You two are considered geniuses at deducing perpetrators behind various minor neighborhood crimes." He shrugged. "Frankly, I don't see why they're so hopped up on you two."

Edge smirked. "Let me ask you a very important question, detective." Aimes gazed at Edge and shrugged a why not. "Did you receive a report of a second murder at the Silakov residence?"

Aimes looked to his partner who shook his head. His eyes narrowed as his gaze fell once again over Edge. "No. Is this some kind of joke?"

Edge snorted. "No joke I'm afraid. Mrs. Stein's daughter Hazy told us she witnessed the murder of Mrs. Silakov."

Aimes exploded in sarcastic laughter and stood up from the couch. "Com'on, Green, let's get the hell outta here." Edge's eyes became deadly serious. "Detective, I think you are making a serious mistake."

"And why would that be?"

"Because I think this time there really has been a murder. In fact, I think the earlier report of a murder was a diversion for the second murder—-the real murder."

Aimes look nonplussed. "I still don't understand—"

"Detective, perhaps we should have Mrs. Stein and her daughter meet us as the Silakov's and we can discuss this with them all. I think what I have to say will be of great interest to all concerned."

Aimes sighed and nodded to Green who pulled his cell phone from an inside pocket of his suit and dialed a number. In his husky voice he said, "Ok." He pressed the end button and put his cell phone back in his inside jacket pocket.

Immediately, I heard the brief wail of a siren from outside and I knew what had happened. The police had been waiting and had finally sprung their trap. The spider had caught the flies before they could escape the web.

***

We arrived at the Silakov's to find a shirtless Ivan Silakov dressed only in worn blue jeans seated on a chocolate brown leather sofa.

Mirror Image

His azure eyes glared at a tall male uniformed police officer who stood over him. Beside him sat a contrite Hazy Stein who, like him, was handcuffed. Her appearance was also disheveled, as if she'd dressed fireman-quick. She wore a man's sleeveless undershirt and gray track pants, her feet were bare, and her toenails were painted fluorescent pink. I was surprised to see her Goth persona had disappeared. Her pink skin was flushed, and her now auburn hair spilled over her bare shoulders. Hazy Stein now looked more like Lindsay Lohan on a day off, than Hazy the Goth girl.

Across the room, seated on a matching leather chair, sat Mrs. Stein her head hung low and her cheeks streaked with spent tears.

Aimes kicked things off. "All right, now that we have everyone present perhaps I will ask Mr. Morton Edge to explain how we all came to be here."

Edge bowed slightly at the waist to acknowledge Detective Aimes. I knew it! They had been in cahoots from the start. I felt a slow burn deep in my gut. Edge had been keeping secrets from me. When this was over he and I were going to have a long talk about where our definitions of partnership diverged.

Right now though, this would have to wait. Edge began to explain.

"First we have the widow Stein." He directed his attention to Mrs. Stein who offered him a weak smile. "Sad as it is Mrs. Stein is the only reliable witness in this entire affair. And she is also the victim of a terrible and tragic fraud—" he paused for dramatic effect. How I hate when he does that-- "perpetrated by her only daughter."

"You're a liar!" Hazy glared daggers at Edge.

Edge ignored her outburst and continued, "Mrs. Stein reported a murder; except when the police arrived they found the supposed victim very much alive. What they didn't know was that Ivan Silakov was most likely already dead."

"You imaginin' things," said Silakov.

"You'll get your turn," cautioned Aimes. "For now, keep your mouth shut." Silakov glared at Aimes his jaw tight and his cheeks flushed. He elected to exercise his right of silence.

Edge said, "We know Mrs. Stein saw a body lying on the living room floor of this house and a woman in a wheelchair wielding a gun because of the daughter Hazy's statement to my colleague. Miss Stein told Razor she saw Mr. Silakov shoot his wife, which in fact he did."

"He lie! I murder no one!" It speaks.

Green moved over and placed one massive hand on Silakov's shoulder. Silakov winced as Green indicated he had better keep silent by applying an apparent Vulcan nerve pinch.

"Detective, you will find the body of the late Mrs. Silakov buried beneath the pile of discarded building materials in the backyard. I had wondered why the Silakov's had fired their remodeling company and abandoned the work until Hazy told Razor about the second murder. It made sense as a temporary hiding place for the body until they could escape with Mrs. Silakov's money. Naturally, Miss Stein would pose as Mrs. Silakov." Edge shook his head his expression sad. The dark side of human nature wore on my friend.

"She would use Mrs. Silakov's wheelchair to disguise the fact she was a healthy young woman. After all, this Mr. Silakov would vouch for his pretend wife. Bank officials would never suspect this Ivan Silakov was in reality his twin brother, Petra."

"But what is Hazy's motive?" I asked inserting myself into Edge's carefully constructed plot. "Why report a second murder? I mean why not just kill Mrs. Silakov and scoop up the money, if that was the plan, then run off with Mr. Silakov?

It's obvious to me given their state of undress that these two are quite fond of one another." Inside I was disappointed. I had grown rather fond of the Goth version of Hazy Stein myself. Evidently, her Goth look was designed to distract me. In that she had certainly succeeded, and ripped my heart out in the process.

"Yes, that would make sense unless, in order to secure Miss Stein's cooperation, her lover was required to stage his own murder. Hazy Stein not only wanted to run off with Mr. Silakov who had become her lover, but she wanted to humiliate her mother even further by making her appear crazy. Her hate for her mother was even stronger incentive than the millions of dollars she would reap."

Hazy glared at Edge but said nothing her lips compressed in a thin line.

Edge continued, "Unfortunately, for Miss Stein I suspect once they were outside the country this Mr. Silakov would have disposed of her as well."

"That not true!" protested Silakov, though his tone suggested otherwise.

Hazy looked at her lover incredulously. "You would kill me?" He simpered at her his eyes pleading innocence. She didn't believe him because she snorted in disgust.

She tore her eyes away from him. "Edge is right. Mila is dead but I didn't kill her—he did," she indicated Silakov. Unable to move his arms, restrained by the handcuffs, he slammed hard against her. Hazy fell off the sofa onto the floor. Before anyone could stop him he began to kick her.

Green moved quickly to restrain him and managed to deflect a vicious kick aimed at her head. "Bitch!" he screamed, "I gonna kill you!" Green smothered the smaller man with his bulk, then lifted him bodily off the sofa and handed him, still struggling, to the uniform that stood watch as if he were a marionette. The uniform wrapped strong dusky fingers around Silakov's left arm and dragged him kicking and screaming from the room. The last I saw of him, he was foaming at the mouth like a rabid dog.

A female uniformed officer with a red ponytail appeared from an adjacent hallway pushing a wheelchair. "I found this in a back bedroom."

Mrs. Stein glared at Hazy. "How could you?"

"It's your fault, mother!" said Hazy. Eloise Stein stared at her daughter clearly horrified that somehow she had been blamed for the murder of an invalid.

"It would have worked too if Edge and Razor hadn't been so smart," said Hazy bitterly. "I hate you all. Especially you mother."

Aimes nodded to Green who helped Hazy up by one arm and led her from the room.

All that was left of her was the scent of her cinnamon tinged perfume.

***

There you have it, the first murder case solved by Razor and Edge Investigations. I suspect now that we have allied ourselves with Detective Aimes this will not be our last.

I am blogging now from Edge's parent's recreation room because, Edge explained, my bedroom was a temporary situation, a kind of social experiment to see if I could keep the room clean. Naturally I failed his test. (Believe me I'm thankful. I've hated cleaning my room since I was seven years old. My mom can attest to this fact.)

Our new headquarters is now his parent's recreation room. I brought an old laptop with me to use while I'm in our office. I'll store it in the hall closet when I'm not using it. (Edge detests technology.)

After Mrs. Stein made her official statement and left for home, Aimes expressed his appreciation for our stick-to-it-ivness.

He explained that when Mrs. Stein reported the first murder and they found the supposed victim alive, he had made some inquires and suspected there was much more to the Silakovs than he had initially thought. Like Edge, his instincts told him something was amiss.

Aimes was kind enough to tell Mrs. Stein that he didn't think she was crazy, and in fact had believed she had seen something unexplained the first time he spoke with her. Good man that Aimes.

It was after midnight when we finished our official statements. By then the police dogs had located the body of Mila Silakov just where Edge said it would be. A search of the Silakov residence revealed two airline tickets to Grand Cayman, though Mr. Silakov's was the only one that was open ended which suggested Edge was right about Silakov's plan to dump Hazy as his excess baggage (with extreme prejudice).

I grappled with Hazy Stein's motives for her heinous acts.

I looked away from the blog entry I'd written but hadn't sent to my blog site yet. "I don't think I'll ever understand the human heart."

Edge placed the book he'd been reading open faced in his lap.

"Love, hate, greed…these are often motivators for murder…" A frown now creased his forehead. "Love is the most painful and volatile emotion in the human repertoire."

"Sad isn't it?" I said and I meant it.

"Yes, Razor—yes it is." Again Edge disappeared behind his book,

I turned back to my blog and typed in the final three sentences.

Friends, it was the mirror image of love that killed Mila Bronovitch. Real love is out there somewhere. Never give up looking for love. I know I never will.

"Did you get Mrs. Stein's check?" Edge said matter-of-factly.

I slapped my forehead. I'd been so engrossed in the mystery I'd forgotten about getting paid. Then I remembered something important.

"Didn't Hazy Stein hire us?" Edge snorted from behind his book. He was right, of course. Now that we'd solved a real murder our future as private detectives was going to take off. The future finally looked bright.

I hit the send button to transmit our case report to our blog then turned off my laptop, stored it in the closet, and headed home to bed.

The Parrot of Doom

I HAD NEVER SEEN A REAL PARROT in the flesh (or should I say in the feather), before today.

From where I sat on the worn leatherette sofa in my partner, Morton Edge's, parents recreation room I stared at the brightly colored green, and yellow (but mostly green) parrot, with a mustard yellow stripe across his beak. The bird sat on a perch in a cage that appeared to be designed to hold the Count of Monte Cristo it was so big.

The parrot (Edge explained his name is Hercules) had been dropped off by a client and we were to interrogate it.

"So what is the parrot supposed to tell us?" I asked.

Edge looked up from the romance novel he'd been reading, his hazel eyes free from emotion. He rarely displays human emotion because he thinks it's a sign of weakness. I think it shows we're all human. I sometimes wonder if Edge is human because he sees the world in such a different way. Then again this is the reason he's so gifted at deductive reasoning, and so bad at human relations.

Human relations is my job at Razor and Edge Investigations. I'm the one who wears out his shoe leather.

"Razor, please refer to the parrot as Hercules. He understands our every word, and I'm told he's offended when referred to as an object."

Objectifying a bird? Now I really have heard everything.

"Huh, yeah, sorry, Hercules," I said, directing my words to the parrot staring back at me with one coal-black eye.

I almost jumped out of my skin when the parrot spoke. "No worries," he said. "Please call me Hercules."

"Uuuuhhh, yeah, OK." My cheeks grew warm. I couldn't believe it but I was embarrassed. I shifted my bony behind on the sagging sofa cushion.

The Parrot of Doom

The darned thing is so old and ratty sometimes the springs press the flesh with the occupant. This old sofa is where the butt meets the road.

I gathered my rattled senses and decided I better speak to the parrot. "So, Hercules, what is it you're supposed to tell us?"

The reply was immediate. He shuffled along the perch farther away from me then said, "About Mr. Cunningham's affair."

Hercules was certainly clear, but I was confused. I'd missed something so I directed my next question to my partner. "Edge, I'm obviously out of the loop, could you perhaps explain what's going on, and why Hercules is here?"

Edge closed his novel, after slipping in a bookmark, then set the book on the end table next to his Barcolounger. "Do you wish to explain, Hercules?"

"After you, Mr. Edge."

Oh, brother. To this day I think Hercules was mocking me.

Edge nodded sagely. "Mrs. Cunningham contacted me asking us to follow her husband because she believed he was being unfaithful. She said she'd pay us any amount we asked for. I explained we do not take those kind of cases."

Though I knew he was right, I was disappointed we'd lost a paying client to a little thing like ethics. I frowned and glanced at the parrot sitting serenely on his perch then back at Edge. "If you refused the case then why is the pa—I mean, Hercules, still here?"

"Because he knows something about Mrs. Cunningham's murder."

To say I was shocked by this revelation would be an understatement of the first magnitude. "What? Mrs. Cunningham is dead? So who brought us the bird?"

"Mr. Cunningham," said the parrot.

I paused to consider the information I had so far. Mrs. Cunningham calls us to hire us to follow her husband who she thinks is having an affair. She is then murdered, and her grieving husband brings us the bird. What? This is nuts.

"But why would Mr. Cunningham bring us the bird?"

Edge shook his head. "He didn't," my partner said matter of factly.

"I called Mr. Edge," said Hercules.

I gawked at the parrot. *He* called Edge?

Edge chuckled. "Sorry, Razor, I've been having too much fun. Please forgive me." He paused and his lips formed a crooked smile.

The Parrot of Doom

"Hercules knew Mrs. Cunningham had called us and pressed the re-dial on the phone. He told me that he'd witnessed Mr. Cunningham killing his wife. He was indeed having an affair, and planned to run off with his lover.

"After Hercules called me I contacted Detective Aimes telling him I had spoken to a witness to a murder, and that the murderer was about to kill the witness."

"Too true," interrupted Hercules.

Edge smiled then continued. "I gave Aimes the address and the police arrived in time to catch Mr. Cunningham attempting to flee, and they saved Hercules from certain death."

"I'm the parrot of doom," said Hercules.

Parrot of doom? Oh, brother. Who knew a parrot could be so dramatic. Then again it would make a good blog title.

"So back to my original question," I said. "Why is he here?"

"The Cunningham's adult daughter is flying in from Los Angeles tomorrow. She'll take Hercules back with her. We're looking after him until then."

"Oh." I eased back against the sofa cushion.

I snatched the TV remote off the scarred pine coffee table in front of the sofa.

"Wanta watch some TV, Edge?

"I like the Home and Garden Network," said Hercules.

I looked at Edge. "Edge?"

He shrugged. "Parrot's choice."

I turned the television on and changed the channel to the Home and Garden Network.

Parrots choice indeed. Stupid parrot's gonna be doomed alright.

String of Pearls

I turned each page of the New Age Heroes comic book slowly, careful not to hum. I wasn't reading it. I was biding my time waiting for Edge to say something, anything really, since I'd entered the room.

Man, was it hot today. The outside temperature had been over ninety every day for the past week. At least his parent's recreation room was below ground so it was a little cooler in here.

As was our custom we met in the faux wood-paneled recreation room. It is the headquarters of The Razor and Edge Detective Agency. As he usually did Edge sat in his Barcalounger recliner spooning rice crisp cereal and milk into his mouth. And as usual I was sitting on the aging gray sofa with the sagging cushions that too often force me to shift my bottom to escape an out of control spring.

On the aluminum TV tray next to his chair lay today's issue of the New York Times with the headline that caused Edge to fall into silence the moment I placed it on the tray.

His grey-green eyes were fixed on a spot on the wall across the room. It was my best friends habit to consider all the known facts before making any verbal observations. Edge has no tolerance for small talk. It had been fifteen minutes and my nerves threatened to overwhelm me unless he spoke soon.

Not that the silence was unusual with Edge.

Morton Edge and I have been friends since we met in the third grade at P.S. 14 Cornelius Vanderbilt grammar school. On the day we met I intervened to stop a bully from threatening to relieve him of his lunch money. Even at that tender age I abhorred crime and the persecution of the weak and the oppressed. Fighting crime was in my blood, especially since both my mother and father are New York County Prosecutors.

Edge, I soon discovered, has a genius intellect and he and I became fast friends after he rewarded me by tutoring me in mathematics, a subject that to this day is not my best.

String of Pearls

Finally, to break the silence I cleared my throat and began to hum a Rodgers and Hammer show tune. I needed his response to the headline. Now anything to break his concentration seemed the right thing to do. I had to know what the next step in our investigation would be.

Edge's concentration now broken he turned toward me and locked me with his cool disapproving gaze. A single eyebrow arched ever so slowly on his forehead. I have experienced this intimidation tactic of his a number of times and it is very unnerving, at least to me. "Razor. Stop. Now."

I stopped humming. I know how much he detests humming, but as I'd intended it re-established the communication link between us.

"Edge, we have to do something about *this*." I pointed to the newspaper headline screaming STRING OF ROBBERIES REMAIN UNSOLVED. "And soon."

The other eyebrow arched on his pale brow. "Why?"

I dropped the comic book on the sofa next to me and rose to my feet determined this time to argue with my brilliant colleague. My Dayton's squeaked softly when I stood upright. I winced. I'd forgotten to treat the leather after the rain of this past weekend. Again. Now Edge would remind me of my error. Again.

After all he is the detail eccentric of our duo. That made him Morton Edge.

I started to pace the room careful not to hit my head on the low ceiling. I thought about asking for the seemingly hundredth time how we were supposed to run a private detective agency from such a place, but Edge would supply his standard response. He'd ask how can one argue with free rent, an unlimited of supply of breakfast cereal, and access to his extensive research library. All true but I'd bumped my head so many times my scalp under my red Mohawk must be perpetually black and blue. It was days like these when I cursed my tall gene.

"This is happening in our backyard. We have to do something." I walked to the basement window and pulled back the thin curtain that covered it. A ray of sunlight streamed across the brown-orange shag carpet that covered the floor. Along with the paneling the carpet had been in stalled in the seventies.

A deep frown marred Edge's forehead and he nodded. "Yes, Razor I agree. We must do something." He paused and his eyes shifted to the door behind which was the stairs to the main floor of his parents house.

A man of twenty-five who still lives at home is truly pathetic.

And I would know, I'm one of them.

"But first I have to go to the library," Edge said with the finality in his tone I knew meant he'd made up his mind.

I crave action. It's why I love most about my role in our investigations.

Two months ago I'd tackled Mr. Simmons when he tried to escape after Edge revealed he had been the person poisoning the neighborhood cats. A few scrapes and bruises later I had him on the ground pinned with his arms behind his back. Before the inevitable confrontation, Edge called Detective Aimes of the 22nd Precinct. He arrived in time to make the arrest. Needless to say Detective Aimes wasn't too pleased to be called to arrest the perpetrator of multiple *kittycides*, until Edge revealed Simmons trade in endangered species including, not surprisingly, a rare species of Finch. It explained why he exterminated cats.

Of course, Edge didn't share this information with me beforehand, something he rarely does, unless I'm going to be in mortal danger. Since I'm not a member of the *Felis domesticus* family he assumed I wouldn't be in any life threatening danger. Regardless, I'd always been able to handle myself when there was a little rough stuff.

Russ Crossley

Recent events foretold of an ill wind blowing through the streets of Staten Island. (Yes, I know it's a bit poetic but after all I majored in nineteenth century English poetry at NYU before my ill-fated switch to law, at Edge's urging. We both dropped out of law school after a year, but that's another story).

A serial cat burglar had been working the neighborhood for the past two months and our neighbor, Mrs. Gold nearly died when she confronted the burglar in her living room.

Mrs. Gold played bridge at her sister's home in Queens on Tuesday's. She left home precisely at six in the evening, returning home at eleven thirty, also precisely.

However, this past Tuesday Mrs. Gold's sister contracted a nasty flu and canceled the game. The newspaper account (I'm naturally summarizing the article for your benefit, dear reader) stated the burglar entered through the kitchen door that opened onto the back garden.

Mrs. Gold attacked the intruder with a straw broom when he entered the living room. After a strenuous battle managed to beat him back into the kitchen.

String of Pearls

Once in the kitchen the criminal grabbed a frying pan off a hook where it hung over the stove and somehow managed to strike Mrs. Gold across the back of her head. She landed on her stomach face down, her head bleeding, seconds away from losing consciousness. The intruder then exited via the kitchen door and disappeared into the gloom of the night.

Fortunately, Mrs. Gold wears a medical alert bracelet and she managed to press the button before she passed out. The ambulance arrived at her home within seven minutes of being alerted by the monitoring station. This fact alone saved her life.

Mrs. Gold currently resides at Staten Island University Hospital with a concussion, bruises and, knowing her as I did, a serious mad-on for the would be thief. No one bested Mrs. Gold and lived to tell the tale. Figuratively, of course.

Before we left Edge and I agreed he would do research at the public library (about what I had no idea) and I would go to the hospital to interview Mrs. Gold.

At this point you should know Edge loathes technology. The Internet is not his tool of choice. He prefers old school research. Books, newspapers, and magazines are his preferred research tools.

Tough to argue with results though.

As I stood on the train station platform my cell phone buzzed. I keep it on silent in my shirt pocket so as not to attract attention from anyone nearby.

Now you can imagine my shock when I flipped it open and saw the number for the Todt Hill-Westerleigh Library. I know you're wondering how I recognize the number. I have called the number many times looking for Edge. It's the one on the desk of the head librarian. Mr. Staple told me never to call his number again so you can imagine my trepidation at seeing his telephone number on the screen.

I picked up the receiver and keyed the green button. "Hello, Mr. Staple?"

"Don't be ridiculous, Razor, it's me Morton Edge."

Edge? I hate it when he uses his full name as if I don't know it.

The tension in my shoulders eased as a sense of relief washed over me. Edge hadn't created the havoc he sometimes did when he visited the library. Once too often he argued the 'facts' in some of the non-fiction books were incorrect. Mr. Staple very nearly banned him when Edge insisted Einstein's theory of relativity was pure fantasy.

I intervened on Edge's behalf and managed to convince Staple my friend was an escaped genius from a special government program for savants. This cover story had thus far held, and I hoped it continued for many years.

"Razor, I believe I have the answer to the robberies."

I didn't even know the question. "And that would be?"

"Do we have a street map of Staten Island? The ones they have here are far too big for my purposes."

"Uhhh, no Edge *we* don't. Why?"

While I was on the question of why I wondered why I was the one asking all the questions and he hadn't yet answered one of them.

"Please pick one up when you return from visiting Mrs. Gold." The line went dead before I could respond. Why did I have to get the map? Another why question with no answer other than the obvious, I was the leg man of our team.

I made a note to contact Royce, leader of the Newspaper Boy League a group who often conduct surveillance operations for us during our investigations.

The league travels the streets and back alleys of the city unnoticed in the early morning hours delivering newspapers. They observe and report back to us when they on all sorts of felons at work. For some reason felons were night birds who skulked about the Big Apple hidden in the shadows.

I don't know what made me think of the Royce at this moment but it seemed a reasonable action. According to the press reports I'd seen the robberies occurred only in the early hours of the day.

The train screamed into the station and as it came to a stop the doors slide open. I stepped on board and the doors quickly closed behind me. I wondered what Edge had discovered that required a street map as the train pulled away from the station.

***

I checked at the registration desk upon entering the hospital for Mrs. Gold's room number. I was grateful the hospital was air-conditioned. Summer in New York can be stifling.

The clerk told me Mrs. Gold's room was on the fourth floor in the geriatric care ward. Not surprising she'd been moved to that particular ward since she had to be over sixty. I'm not sure exactly how old Mrs. Gold was but she appears to be older than my parents who are in their forties.

My parents are also lawyers.

Before I took the elevator to the fourth floor I stopped in the gift shop to select a spray of flowers in a glass vase as a get well gift.

In the PI trade we call this greasing-the-wheels.

A gift loosens the tongue in order to gain more detailed information in addition to what had appeared in the newspaper. While the police were sure to have questioned her already Edge and I can take liberties the police cannot. And we can use other sources and tactics to discover the perpetrator the official authorities cannot.

After Mrs. Gold my next visit would be to Detective Aimes. I planned my route such that I'd pass the tourist information office where I'd secure a map for Edge. I still had no idea why he needed a map, but I'd learned from experience Edge had his reasons and, from experience, it's best to acquiesce to his requests without too many questions. Naturally, I'd never see the money for the price of the map but that as they say is the cost of doing business.

The door to Mrs. Gold's room was closed when I arrived so I rapped gently before I went to enter.

"Yes? Who is it?"

"It's me, Mrs. Gold, Jerome Saperstein."

I used my real name with Mrs. Gold since she had known me long before I became Goth and now went by the name Razor.

When I was ten she used to bake cookies for us neighborhood kids. My mouth still watered when I thought about those cookies.

"Jerome?" she sounded surprised.

"May I come in?"

"Oh, of course, Jerome. Please come in."

I turned the handle then pushed the door in with one hand went to enter. It startled me when someone pushed back. I stepped back and a tall, thin man wearing as brown suit jacket and, white shirt and dark pants pushed back and almost ran over me as he was coming out. He didn't look like a doctor to me.

"Hi," I said in my most friendly tone hoping it would elicit an introduction. Instead the man scowled at me, his lips formed a grim line, then he pushed past me and was gone. As he passed me I noticed a tattoo of a falcon with its wings extended on his neck.

Strange fellow. I shirked off the encounter and let out a breath. I was just here to pay a visit to an injured neighbor, and to ask a few questions, not to meet her family.

String of Pearls

A person with a concussion usually has excruciating headaches hence the lighting is often subdued until the patients headache recedes. But then again what do I know I'm a law school drop out not a doctor.

The room had two beds the one closer to the windows was unoccupied. Mrs. Gold sat propped up in the bed by pillows with the covers half way up her chest. A bandage was wrapped around her skull and her grey eyes twinkled at me when I walked in.

Her bow wrinkled slightly as I showed her the glass vase with the two flowers in it. "Jerome, you didn't have to bring me anything. Sorry about my nephew, Barney. He's always been a little brusque with people he doesn't know. He seems to think everyone I know is after my money." She forced a chuckle. "As if I have any."

I hadn't expected an explanation about the thin man with the bad attitude. I waved off her apology as if it was nothing and smiled. "No worries, Mrs. Gold. We're neighbors after all."

"Yes, of course." She sighed. "Sad that it takes me getting a bump on the noggin for you and I to get together these days."

I nodded and looked around to find a chair to sit on while we talked.

I found a navy blue plastic chair on the other side of the bed nearer to the window and carried it the side of Mrs. Gold's hospital bed. I sat down and studied her. Her beady eyes were sunken and surrounded by dark circles. She smiled weakly.

"It's nice of you to visit me," she began. I set the flower vase on her rolling bedside table. "Those flowers are lovely. Thank you."

I nodded again uncertain how to begin. "So, Mrs. Gold how're you doing?" I cringed inside. I must sound like a moron.

"Other than the worst headache in history, and my entire body feels like its been run over by a steamroller, I'm fine. Thank goodness my late husband had good health insurance."

"When are you getting out?"

"Tomorrow. They're releasing me tomorrow."

I folded my hands in my lap. I wanted to fidget but I restrained myself. I don't care for hospitals. They're full of sick people. "That's nice."

Mrs. Gold watched me in silence her eyes narrowing slightly. My urge to squirm grew exponentially with each passing second of silence between us. Good thing hospital rooms don't have ticking clocks or I'd have gone crazy for sure.

"Why are you really here, Jerome?" she said at last.

I never could fool her. There was no point in trying to lie or dodge the question. She'd known me almost since the crib. I cleared my throat. "Edge and I are investigating the string of break-ins in the neighborhood. I'm here because I'd like to ask you if there's anything you recall about the attack that might help us."

Her brow wrinkled. "I already told the cops everything. You should ask them."

If I knew the police they were too busy to bother with a few B and E's. They'd have already put the file to bed. If someone on my block owned the Hope Diamond then they'd be interested. But since no one I know was swimming in cash I don't think the cops will be investigating any time soon.

"I'm going to see Detective Aimes later."

Her eyes widened then retreated as she nodded. "Oh, good. He'll clear everything up." Her hands had begun to tremble and I saw the fear in her eyes.

Now that caught my attention. Mrs. Gold was afraid. To say I was shocked is an understatement of the nth magnitude. This development worried me. Fear was out of character for Mrs. Gold to be afraid.

Mrs. Gold's parents survived the holocaust so there was very little that frightened her. What could it be that was so bad?

Nothing about this case made sense.

I sensed her reluctance to share what was bothering her. She'd never tell me whatever had scared even under torture, and I certainly wasn't going to torture her. I had to give up, for now.

I patted her trembling arm laying above the bed covers. "Thanks, Mrs. Gold. You get some rest and come home soon, okay?"

She smiled warmly. "Tomorrow. They're sending me home tomorrow."

I grinned sheepishly. "Yes, of course. Sorry, I forgot."

***

I arrived at the steps to the front doors of the Twenty Second Precinct forty minutes later. I wiped the sweat from my brow then climbed the steps two at a time. Two uniformed male cops exited the twin front doors just as I came to the top step. As usually happens when a Goth enters a police station they glared at me. Uniformed cops by definition are conformists. Uni, meaning one, and form as in they all take one form dislike rebels like me.

I ignored them and walked straight to the reception desk. Wendy Sandhu was behind the desk. A frown darkened her already light brown features when she spotted me coming toward her. I, on the other hand, forced a cheery how's-hangin'-girl smile on my face.

People can always see if a so-called sincere smile is fake. It's in the eyes. An insincere smile never makes it to the eyes. I had practiced fake smiles in the mirror for hours so I could make it seem I'm sincere. You never knew what little things will come in handy in the PI business.

"Hey, Wendy." I greeted her cheerily. "Good to see you. Is Detective Aimes in?" With Wendy I avoid small talk whenever possible. She hates small talk.

"What do you want with Detective Aimes?"

"I'm helping him because, as you know, I'm helpful." I leaned an elbow on the reception counter and winked at her.

She rolled her eyes and pressed a button on the consol in front of her. I heard the muffled reply from her headset. "Sir, there's a young man to see you." She scowled at me. "Yes, sir it's Razor," she added after a brief pause.

Suddenly her expression eased and she shrugged. "Ok, detective whatever you say."

She shook her head. "I'll never understand that man," she said under her breath.

"Problem?"

She locked eyes with me and made me feel like butter left on the counter in the heat of summer.

"No, nothing. Detective Aimes will see you." Her tone was heavy with sarcasm.

"Thanks. No need to show me the way. I know where his office is." Not that Aimes has an office per se. He refers to the fourth floor filled with rows of ancient wooden desks as the bull pen. This was where the overworked detectives of robbery homicide of the 22nd precinct are housed.

I arrived on the fourth floor to be met at the elevators by a disheveled Aimes. He hustled me into an interview room and I sat at the single chair facing him. He had a manila file folder with him. Not that I was worried. I'm sure he didn't want his colleagues to see us together.

Imagine the headline, Goth Kid Saves Police Bacon.

"Razor," he began, "Good to see you."

"What's the problem?" I said assuming there was a problem.

String of Pearls

"My boss won't let us loose on the string of robberies in your neighborhood, even with the assault against Mrs. Gold."

"So what do you want me to do?" I asked.

Aimes slapped the folder on the table then ran a hand through his dark curly hair. I noticed his light blue dress shirt looked like it'd been slept in and his chiseled features were darkened by stubble. His eyes were red, common to someone suffering from lack of sleep. The guy looked stressed to the max.

He stopped and placed both hands flat on the table. He leaned toward me and stared. "I'm going to leave this folder on the table for ten minutes while I go to the can. When I come back the folder better be here and you better be gone. Do we understand each other?"

I smiled thinly. "Perfectly."

***

I arrived home with the map as requested. I found Edge seated in his usual lounger with a stack of papers in his lap. His brown eyes were focused as he concentrated on the current page.

As I sat down on the sofa I caught a glimpse of the page he was reading and saw it was a newspaper article complete with a picture of a young woman dressed in a navy blue business suit.

She wore a thin layer of make up that accented her high cheek bones. Her dirty blonde, hair that cascaded about her shoulders was perfectly cut and styled, indicating a person of means who attended the best salons. By her appearance I deduced she was a professional woman, probably a lawyer, or a publishing executive, or an accounting firm vice president, or some equally well compensated profession.

"Hello, Edge. I'm back." He grunted in response but otherwise ignored me. "I have the map you asked for."

This caused him to look up from the newspaper article he'd been reading. "Good, Razor. Very good. Report."

Report means I tell him everything I've done investigating the case. I once tried to slip in a joke—something about bodily functions as I recall—Edge wasn't amused so I never tried it again.

I told him about my conversation with Mrs. Gold, and nearly running into her nephew. I left nothing out even my suspicion about her fear and her nervous manner. And I described the tattoo on the nephew's neck as he walked past me.

Edge listened thoughtfully until I finished.

After several seconds of silence he finally said, "Get the card table from the hall closet. I have a theory about these crimes."

I got up and retrieved the card table as instructed. I set it up in the middle of the room.

I was anxious to hear Edge's theory of the crime. He's a brilliant detective who analysis' all the facts and then identifies the perpetrator in front of the whole room filled with suspects. He's a little old fashioned that way but it usually works to unmask a villain and elicit a confession.

After the table was set up Edge stood and moved to stand beside it while I spread out the map of Staten Island.

Edge frowned at the map then glanced at me. "Is this the best you could find?"

"I'm sorry, Edge but this is all the tourist office had. I can visit a topography office tomorrow if you wish and get a more detailed one." Frankly I was puzzled. The map depicted all of the streets, parks and key points of interest. I thought it a rather good map.

"No matter, Razor. This will have to do." I was relieved then and knew I had done well. Edge was only being theatrical.

Edge studied the map carefully as his brow furrowed and his eyes traveled the streets and back alleys of the neighborhoods that make up Staten Island. Finally his features relaxed and he pulled out a felt tipped marker from his shirt pocket then drew an elliptical circle that encompassed certain houses on streets that seemed familiar. I recognized one house that could very well be Mrs. Gold's.

Edge nodded as he finished and made that satisfying sigh-whistle through his nose he does when he's solved a picture puzzle, or a criminal case.

Before he could say anything I went to retrieve the laptop computer I kept in a case in a corner of the room for just such instances as this. I pulled my cell phone from my pocket. It's memory card contained the pictures of the pages from the folder Aimes had left with me knowing I would photograph them.

I set the lap top up on a TV tray and booted it up. The photos downloaded within seconds.

I looked over my shoulder. Edge had retreated to his beloved Barcalounger and sat staring at the wall, his brow creased by deep thoughts as he processed his own data.

I picked up the laptop and cradled under one arm and carried it to the chair next to Edge's chair. I sat down showed him the first photo.

It contained a list of house addresses that had been robbed in the past two months. He remained silent but his eyes shifted to look at the page on the screen.

"Edge these are the addresses of the break-in victims. And there's more." I tapped the enter key and the next photo appeared. "And this is a list of the victim's names.

"And the *piece de resistance*." I tapped the enter key again. A third page appeared. "A list of stolen items."

A single eyebrow rose on Edge's forehead and his eyes narrowed as he studied the page. Finally his face relaxed and I knew.

The final piece of the puzzle had just fallen into place. It was time to bring in the suspects.

***

Detective Aimes knows Edge is a very good detective. We have solved several cases together so when I called and asked him to invite a list of names Edge gave me to meet us in Edge's parents recreation room he agreed after only a few seconds deliberation. I could hear in his voice his usual reluctance. Aimes always asks if he can invite them to the 22nd, but Edge always insists they come here. It was their little game and Edge always won.

Seated in the recreation room looking extremely uncomfortable were Mrs. Gold and her nephew, Barney.

For some reason he didn't look like an Barney, but then my name is Razor so who am I to talk? His reedy, whiny voice was really getting to me and he'd only been here for ten minutes.

"My aunt has *just* been released from the hospital, officer," he complained once again to Aimes.

"It's Detective, Mr. Brilberg and your attendance here is strictly voluntary. You may leave at any time," replied Aimes in his professional police monotone.

In the first run through of this little drama nephew Barney suggested to his aunt they leave immediately. Mrs. Gold swallowed hard and her knuckles were white from gripping her hand bag strap so tightly. She refused to leave explaining Edge and I were her friends and she wanted to stay. The fear in her eyes was almost palpable.

Barney opened his mouth to speak then looked at me scowled and his mouth snapped shut. He seemed to be very irritated.

Edge sat regal-like in his chair his dark eyes flitting between the two. Finally he turned his head to face Royce. When I'd seen the young man walk into the room I silently cursed myself.

I'd forgotten to call him. Obviously, Edge had
noted my error and had not only contacted Royce but
asked him to come to the unveiling of the perpetrator.

"Royce," began Edge, "please tell Detective
Aimes what you told me."

"Yes, sir, Mr. Edge." The boy smiled at me.

"Like I told ya, me and the boys seen a man
dressed in dark clothing near all them streets where
the robberies happened. He was tall and skinny, kinda
like Mr. Brilberg." Barney glared at the boy but he
continued. "Anyway, one of the guys saw the guy
in black leaving through the back door of one of the
houses that was robbed."

Edge regarded the boy with a steady clear-eyed
gaze. "Did he also fit the description of Mr. Brilberg?"

"Yeah, I guess so. At least that's what the guy
said."

Barney grunted. "They're hundreds, if not
thousands of people who fit my physical description."
His voice was pure sneer.

Edge nodded. "Yes, of course, Mr. Brilberg I
agree. But what not too many men have that you do is
the falcon tattoo on your neck."

It was then I realized Barney was wearing a
turtleneck sweater. The sweat trickling down my
back told me it wasn't exactly turtleneck weather.

He rolled down the left side of the sweater to reveal a pale neck. No tattoo.

I laughed and everyone looked at me. Barney's pale features turned bright crimson and he glared daggers at me.

"The tattoo is on the right side of his neck," I explained.

Suddenly Barney jumped cat-like to his feet. He reached down and pulled a long bladed knife hidden under his right pant leg secured by a strap. His features were pinched and his dark eyes leered at me as he moved to his left the knife ready to slice me like a brisket. He took a step toward me.

My eyes were fixated on the blade. I swallowed hard and my heart pounded fast in my chest. My pulse quickened when he lunged at me swinging the knife left to right barely missing me in the process. He was going to kill me.

"Don't," said a steady, deep voice to my right. I quickly glanced to my right and saw Aimes had his Glock pointed at Barney and he was in a shooting stance.

Whoa. I swallowed hard. I hope he's a good shot.

"Mr. Brilberg, please put down the knife or Detective Aimes will shoot you." It was Edge. Now I was really worried.

If he said anything this guy didn't like I'd be sliced like a Sunday roast.

I saw Barney's features relax and he dropped the knife. Aimes came up behind him and grabbed him the collar of his sweater and shoved him into the wall beside me.

Barney assumed the position, as they say in the movies, then Aimes quickly frisked him then had the handcuffs on before I started to breath again.

After he had him cuffed Aimes gripped Barney by his right arm and guided him to sit in the chair again.

Edge looked at me and grinned. "Well done, Razor."

I stared at my friend and wondered what I had done. "What are you talking about?"

"Why, Razor I'm surprised. You've singlehandedly unmasked the perpetrator behind the string of robberies around the neighborhood, of course." He spoke as if this fact were obvious to everyone in the room.

Aimes eyed Edge and a frown creased his brow. "Perhaps you should explain, Edge." At least I wasn't alone in my confusion.

"Of course," said Edge.

He cleared his throat then we listened in rapt attention as he wove a tale of murder, robbery and kidnapping unlike any I have ever heard.

In his research at the library Edge discovered Barney Brilberg was indeed Mrs. Gold's nephew, but he had been kidnapped while on holiday in Mexico by a drug gang called *Halcones de la muerte* or Falcons of Death.

Gang members must tattoo an image of an attacking falcon on their neck. Barney was most likely dead and this man was an impostor masquerading as Barney.

At the news her nephew was dead, Mrs. Gold covered her face with her hands and began to sob.

Edge stood and moved to her side then placed a hand on her shoulder. "I'm sorry, Mrs. Gold but these gangs are vicious killers with little regard for human life. I know they told you he was alive but I fear the worst."

Edge turned to face the pseudo nephew. "Isn't that correct?"

The man glared daggers at Edge but slowly nodded. He knew his disguise had been compromised so there was no use in pretending ignorance. He also knew cooperation might be useful when he needed bargaining chips with the DA.

It also meant he wasn't a full member of the falcons he was a local recruit. A Mexican gang member would die before he'd talk to the police.

With his pale complexion he obviously wasn't Mexican or Latino so this made perfect sense.

"Why don't you tell us your real name, my friend," said Edge his eyes intense.

The fake nephew's shoulders slumped and his gaze dropped to the worn carpet as he hung his head in defeat. "Ricky Hebert. And, yes I did those robberies." He grimaced. "But I'm not saying anything else without a lawyer."

Edge only nodded. His features bore the smug look I know so well. He moved back to the lounger. When he sat down the cushion sighed. He then placed his arms flat on the chair arms.

"Mr. Herbert is the reason we are all sitting here. He is the perpetrator of the robberies." Edge paused for dramatic effect. "But he is not the mastermind behind these crimes."

Ricky scowled at Edge but remained silent.

Edge shook his head. "No, the mastermind is the leader of *Halcones de la muerte*. A man named known only as Carlos."

Aimes' brow wrinkled. "Yes, it makes sense.

But why would Carlos take a chance by having an operative breaking into houses in New York?"

One side of Edge's mouth curled upward. "He was after something. Something Carlos coveted beyond money or power. He did it for love."

I couldn't help myself, I scoffed. "What! Edge, this time you've gone too far. Love? Who does that but some love sick dolt in those romance books you read."

I stole a glance at Ricky and realized Edge had hit a nerve. Ricky's cheeks were as red as a fire engine. Oh, brother. Love?

"That may be my old friend but nonetheless it is a fact."

"And how did you learn of this *fact*?" said Aimes.

"During my research I discovered in 2009 the very rare Baroda Pearls natural pearls, one of the most valuable strings of pearls in the world, valued at seven million dollars, was stolen and believed sold to a private collector."

"It turns out before he left New York, Carlos stole the pearls as a gift for his wife. He instructed Ricky to smuggle them out of the country for him because he and his belongings would be thoroughly searched prior to exiting.

"Unfortunately for him the pearls were intercepted in a DEA sting operation and sold at auction to a buyer right here on Staten Island. The buyer's name was kept secret, but someone inside the auction house sold Mr. Herbert here the zip code of the buyer and he hoped to get in good with his boss. He's been breaking into to houses trying to find the necklace ever since."

"But what about the assault on Mrs. Gold?" said Aimes obviously warming to Edge's theory, but I think he wasn't buying it for a second. The come-on-get-on-with-it tone in his voice was a dead give away.

"Ricky beat Mrs. Gold to frighten her into agreeing to let him use the house as a base of operations after he told her they had her nephew."

Edge glanced at Mrs. Gold who's features sagged and her cheeks glowed red. "She told the police and the newspaper she was a robbery victim the same as the others to explain her injuries."

Aimes grunted. "Now how do you know that?"

Edge's lips formed a tight smile. "As you recall, detective she told you her sister had the flu." Aimes nodded.

"I contacted Mrs. Gold's sister and discovered Mrs. Gold cancelled the bridge game not her sister.

She told her sister she'd slipped and fallen in the bathtub." Edge eyed Mrs. Gold and she averted her eyes.

"Unfortunately, this was a strategic error on her part because her sister insisted she go to the hospital to get checked out. Knowing her sister abhors the news she was confident her sister would never know when she called the police to report a robbery."

Aimes crossed his arms and frowned. "But how do you know she wasn't robbed?"

"If you look at the list of stolen items you will see hers is the only house where nothing was taken," explained Edge.

Aimes cocked an eyebrow but pulled a copy of the list from the inside pocket of his suit jacket and scanned down the list. His eyes widened as he reached the bottom. "You're right."

Aimes shoved the list back in his pocket and looked at Mrs. Gold. "Is this true ma'am?"

She looked at Ricky then back at Aimes. Her eyes were watery. She nodded.

Aimes pursed his lips then looked at Edge. "Carry on, Edge."

My friend nodded and a small but triumphant smile passed over his lips.

"I believe this supports the idea Ricky was threatening to harm Mrs. Gold's nephew and I think his goal was to retrieve those pearls but for some reason he was running out of time."

"It was my fault," Ricky blurted. "Carlos assigned me to get those pearls out of New York but I messed up and the DEA found them. I got greedy and hid them in a kilo of marijuana." He looked at Aimes. They have sniffing dogs ya know."

Ricky hung his head. "If he finds out what happened I'm dead."

Aimes rolled his eyes and wrapped his fingers around Ricky's arm and brought him to his feet. "Com'on, Ricky let's go talk to the DA." He eyed Edge. "Let's see if we can make a deal."

Ricky smiled. I liked him better when he looked angry. "That'd be nice."

After they were gone Mrs. Gold rose to her feet and moved to stand beside Edge. "Thank you, Morton." Her eyes brimmed with tears. "I was so afraid. Did I do anything wrong?"

Edge smiled kindly at her and shook his head. "No, Mrs. Gold you are the victim here. Ricky lied you so you'd protect him while he searched for the pearls. Now you go home and get some rest."

She nodded and gave him a weak smile then left the room. The last I heard of her were her foot steps disappearing up the stairs. The next day she would move in with her son William and his family. He was a dentist in Scarsdale. She'd been too afraid to tell him what was going on for fear they'd hurt him too.

When Edge and I were alone I sat on the worn sofa and looked at him in his chair. He looked smug and I detest smug.

"Tell me something, Edge?'

"Yes, Razor?"

"It sounds to me like when you were at the library you used the internet to do some of your research."

A sly smiled played over his lips and his eyes twinkled. "I'm going upstairs to get a bowl of cereal. Do you want some?" I shook my head. He rose to his feet and started toward the stairs.

"This is gonna make one heck of a blog entry," I muttered under my breath.

Edge stopped and turned to face me. "Did you say something, Razor?"

"Yes. I was saying I think I'll call this case String of Pearls in my blog."

Edge smiled and nodded. "Yes, that sounds about right." He turned and disappeared up the stairs.

The Kidnapping of Billy Buttons

I LOOKED UP FROM THE COMPUTER SCREEN where I'd been shopping online at the coolgothclothing. com website at the sound of footsteps on the stairs from over head alerted me someone was coming. Until now I was alone in my partner Morton Edge's parents basement recreation room. I didn't wish to be bothered in my quest for cool duds, but if this was a paying client it would also be cool to have the cash to buy the cool clothes.

Soon Edge appeared followed by a red haired kid who looked no more than twelve or thirteen years old.

The kid's pale face was a mass of freckles, and behind his wire-rimmed glasses his eyes were a brilliant blue that seemed to pierce me to my soul. I felt oddly uneasy under his intense gaze.

"Razor, this is Skip Weezer, he needs our help," said Edge. There is no drama in Edge so this was a surprisingly dramatic statement for my best friend and PI partner.

I closed the lap top then set it on the scarred coffee table in front of the new sofa I was sitting on and stood to greet Skip. Kids his age don't shake hands so I didn't make the offer.

I smiled, "Hey, Skipper, how're ya doin'?"

Skip looked at Edge who'd just sat in his Barcalounger. "Is he for real, sir?"

Sir? I realized I'd been had. I had a couple of nephews about his age and they didn't talk like this kid. Edge chuckled at my discomfort.

"Please sit on the sofa, Skip, my partner's manners may not be refined, but he's a competent detective I assure you," said Edge dryly.

Competent? That's all? Anyone who reads this blog knows I'm one of the best PI's in the business.

"What's with the costume?" Skip asked eyeing me with obvious suspicion. The sofa cushion sighed as he settled on the shiny leatherette.

I cocked an eyebrow at Edge to let him know I wasn't pleased with his characterization of me as merely competent, and for his assertion I wasn't <u>refined</u>.

The Kidnapping of Billy Buttons

As if he's anymore refined than me. *Puleeeease.*

We're both born and raised Staten Island-ites, we attended the same grammar school, and we both dropped out of NYU Law School after the first year to start Razor and Edge Private Investigations.

I went to end of the sofa, farthest from our new client, and sat down. It was difficult for me to see a paycheck coming from a kid this age. I hoped Edge wasn't doing another freebie. He does that sometimes, when a case particularly intrigues him.

Skip was dressed in tan cargo pants, basketball shoes, and sporting a forest green tee shirt obviously a size too large for his lean frame since it looked like a tent on him. His clothing was clean, but not expensive, and his carrot-colored hair was trimmed short. To me he didn't look like a bank CEO or a coffee shop owner so he clearly wasn't rolling in green. And he smelled of Captain Crisp cereal, an odor I knew well given all Edge ever eats is sugary breakfast cereal.

"It's not a costume—"Edge began, before I interrupted him.

"The look is called Goth," I finished for him. "It's a lifestyle choice." I smiled knowingly at Edge. He wore a silly grin on his face, which unnerved me more than the kid staring at me.

Something was rotten with this picture.

The kid snorted. "Okay, if you say so."

I dropped the smile and my cheeks grew warm. "Edge, is Skip a client, or long lost relative?"

Edge smirked. "Client." He shifted his gaze to our young client. "Skip, why don't you tell Razor about your problem."

Skip looked at me, his features calm, with a earnestness that belied his tender years. "My teddy bear has been kidnapped."

***

Skip explained the teddy bear (the bears name was apparently Billy Buttons) in question had once been the property of King Robert the Third of Rogberg, a tiny but ancient Kingdom bordered by Italy, France, and Switzerland.

(I made a mental note to locate the country on map. Skip said the country had about five thousand citizens living in an area of sixty acres, and their major industry was a bobble head factory.)

"So who kidnapped the bear?" I asked.

Skip rolled his eyes. "If I knew that I wouldn't need you would I?"

I smiled. You had to love the amateurs. They only understand crime by what they see on television.

The Kidnapping of Billy Buttons

"Kidnappings usually come from two sources: persons, usually professional criminals, who see a way to make a quick buck, or a relative of the *kidnapee* who seeks revenge for some slight real or imagined. So, I'd say, Skipper, you need us more than you think." I paused to consider something else. "Why didn't you go to the police?"

Skip's eyes shied away from mine and his shoulders sagged. I'd gotten under his skin, now I'd be driven to the heart of this case.

Skip rested his hands in his lap and I noticed him intertwining his fingers. "My father is an international financier, he travels a lot."

There was an edge of bitterness in his tone. "Your father has a collection of antique teddy bears," I said. He nodded. "Some of his acquisitions are not *on the books* as we say. Correct?" He nodded again. I stole a glance at Edge his expression revealed he was impressed with my technique. I smiled then turned my attention back to the boy.

Skip nodded. '"Yes. Sir."

Sir? How old does he think I am? "And you were supposed to set the alarm or something, and because you didn't someone broke in and stole Billy Buttons. Right?"

"Yeah. Something like that."

For the first time he sounded more like a boy his age. I felt for him since I remember being his age when every mistake was amplified ten fold from reality. "Have you touched anything where the bear was kept since the robbery?" Edge interjected.

"No, sir, I haven't."

"Good," said Edge. "Razor will go with you to your house and look over the scene of the crime. He will need to dust for prints, though I expect there will be none. And if there are then I suspect the police will have a record of them."

The boy's face turned very pale and his now watery eyes were wide with fear. "The police? You can't tell the police." His voice trembled and he appeared about to start to cry.

I winced. I really hate it when women or little kids cry. I never know what to do. Can you say awkward moments? In the seventh grade Betty Fienberg started crying after she skinned her knee on the playground. I had nightmares for a week.

The corners of Edge's mouth curled up. "Don't be concerned. Razor and I have a reliable contact in the police department. I assure you we will not mention any names." He shrugged slightly. "If we tell him we're helping a little boy find his lost teddy bear I'm certain he won't be too concerned."

The Kidnapping of Billy Buttons

Detective Aimes at the 22nd precinct wasn't going to be too happy to help identifying fingerprints for a lost teddy bear, but he'd helped us with other weird cases so why not this? Since we'd helped him close some difficult cases he owed us.

I rose from the sofa and went to the closet near the door to the staircase leading upstairs to retrieve my long leather coat. I pulled it on and ran a hand through my spiked hair to ensure it was all in place.

Satisfied I look too cool, I turned around to face the sofa to see Skip looking unhappy to be going anywhere with me. I fought to maintain a calm exterior. Prejudice is a terrible thing.

***

The taxi dropped us off in front of a brownstone on West 71st on the Upper West side. The façade was composed of white stone with a cement staircase leading to a shiny black door.

"Is this home?" I asked, wondering to myself why a Goth kid from Staten Island was standing outside a very expensive townhouse in a very exclusive neighborhood. From the stares of people walking by us it appeared Skip's neighbors felt the same. One lady walking her rat-sized dog carrying what smelled like a lavender latte screwed up her face as if she'd just smelled garbage for the first time.

(Which would be true for the wealthy residents in this zip code.)

"Yeah," replied Skip unenthusiastically.

"Nice."

"Yeah."

Skip lead the way up the stairs to the front door. He took a key from his pocket and unlocked the door and we stepped inside. He closed the door while I scanned the interior.

The floor was covered with beautiful tan-colored wood. The furniture was also wood the color matched the floor. The look was rustic and reminded me of a cabin in the woods somewhere. There were stairs that led to the upper floors open, with handrails on both sides, to one side of room near a long wooden table surrounded by chairs. Along one wall was a floor to ceiling built in bookcase interrupted by a built in desk near the middle.

The room was warm and inviting, it conjured up an image of the sophisticated residents who read books by the fire while sipping herbal tea. Since there was not a spot of green growing things anywhere in evidence I suspected this was a man-cave, and my new clients mother had gone to her reward some time in the past. A twinge of regret filtered through my consciousness. Poor kid had lost his mom.

The Kidnapping of Billy Buttons

This realization made me appreciate my own mother even more. Not that I see a lot of my mom or dad since they are both lawyers who work long hours.

"Nice," I said again.

I had to stop myself from laughing when Skip replied with another, "Yeah."

I took off my coat and threw it across the back of one of the chairs in a sitting area in front of a hooded fireplace.

I sniffed the air. Was that roast chicken I smelled? My stomach growled. *Yup, it's chicken.*

"Ah, Herr Razor, I presume?" I turned to see a woman with blonde hair streaked with gray standing in an archway leading to a hallway. Her lack of even a remote resemblance to Skip told me she was the housekeeper for those times when Skip's father was absent.

Her gray hairs, baggy one-size-fits-all plain powder blue dress, and sad, but expressive eyes confirmed my suspicion.

"Hello, Ms...?"

"Helga Schulz, from Dusseldorf. I'm the housekeeper."

I smiled and shook hands with her. Her grip was warm and surprisingly strong. When she smiled the lines at the side of her eyes deepened.

This was one happy German lady who loves to laugh.

"You were expecting me?"

"Yah, Skip, tells me you are helping a friend of his with homework. His friend is doin' a report for school on the Goth peoples."

I maintained the smile on my lips as best I could, but managed to shoot a disapproving glare at Skip when Helga looked away toward the kitchen.

Helga emitted a throaty laugh. "No problem for me. In Germany we have lots of Goth peoples." She chuckled as she walked away headed of the open design kitchen at the far end of the room where the roasting-hen-yummy odor where still coming from.

"Com'om, Razo—" Skip hesitated his expression reflecting his discomfort with my name. "Com'on," he said finally. He started up the stairs and I went after him.

As we reached the next floor Helga's voice drifted up the stairwell after us. "I'll call you boys when dinner is ready."

Skip looked at me and rolled his eyes. He then leaned over the railing that guarded the stairwell. "Thank you, Helga."

He stepped back and shrugged. "She takes pretty good care of me when Dad is away."

The Kidnapping of Billy Buttons

"So I can see." The walls of the room we were standing in were lined with glass display cases containing glass shelves upon which sat a collection of teddy bears that made me think we were being invaded by stuffed animals from another planet. His father's collection was impressive.

The floor was covered with the same wood as the downstairs, and it was spotless. The display cases looked clean as well and free from dust or fingerprints. Each one had a light inside to highlight its down-stuffed occupant. All those blank, beady eyes staring unblinkingly back at you can be unsettling. A whisper of air from the air conditioner in the ceiling brushed against my cheek. I suspected the room was humidity controlled as well. The way these teddy bears were displayed meant they were very valuable.

Each display case had a small white tag in the front below the teddy bear. Each card had a two to thee line description of its occupant.

Every case was occupied. I walked along the row of cases until I came to the one with the name card that read Billy Buttons, Once The Property of Prince Robert of Rogberg. I turned to look at Skip and cocked one eyebrow. "The bear is here."

Skipper avoided my gaze by staring at the floor. He reminded me of a kid with his hand caught in the cookie jar. Been there, done that.

"No, sir, I put in a fake so Helga wouldn't call my father."

"Oh. Makes sense I guess." I turned back to the case and stepped closer. One the left side was a key lock and the glass appeared to have been cleaned recently. In fact, if my nose was right, I detected the faint odor of window cleaner.

"I thought you said you'd left the scene of the crime untouched?"

"Except for placing a fake bear inside, and Helga cleaning the glass outside the case, I have. Tomorrow she'll be cleaning the inside of the cases. Helga has a very precise schedule. She never deviates from her cleaning schedule." He avoided my inquisitive gaze. "That's why dad likes her so much."

I smiled to myself. Poor kid's life was under the thumb of his housekeeper. "Yeah," I said, "I've had a few babysitters in my day who were pretty tough too."

Skip's eyes shot up from staring at the floor to nail me with a glare. "I don't need a babysitter. I'm twelve and three quarters old. I'm not a child." He spat the words and his pale cheeks were cherry red.

The Kidnapping of Billy Buttons

Without meaning to I'd pushed his buttons. "Take it easy, Skip. I didn't mean anything by it."

His features relaxed. "Uhh…sorry. Do you want to see the inside of Billy's display case?" he asked, to obviously avoid the current subject.

I nodded. Skip walked up to the case with the Billy Buttons card and pulled a key from his pocket. He swung open the door to the case then Skip removed the fake bear and stepped aside. I wasn't happy he'd moved it but I didn't wish to upset a very edgy kid.

I stepped closer in order to study the inside of the case for clues. I immediately smelled the same glass cleaner and knew I'd find nothing. This meant Helga had changed her schedule the only question was why?

***

I've learned—sometimes the hard way—to never jump to conclusions during an investigation. This case was no exception.

I stood in the shadows of a darkened doorway across the street for Skip's house waiting for Helga to leave. I'd waited two days for her scheduled visit with her nephew in Queens. I pressed the button on my digital Timex and in the soft glow from the watch face I saw it was nearing seven in the evening.

I preferred using a watch to avoid casting too much light thereby attracting attention by flipping open my cell phone. The light from my phone was far too bright.

I shivered in the fall breeze and pulled up the collar of my leather coat to try to keep warm, and I buried my hands deep in the pockets. An early winter was in the air and I could see my breath.

The front door of Skip's townhouse opened. Helga came out dressed in a gray tweed overcoat with a basket over one arm. When she got to the bottom of the stairs she looked both ways then started walking quickly south away from the nearest subway station. She wasn't heading for Queens.

I followed at a discreet distance. Helga surprised me when she suddenly stopped and I was forced to duck into a doorway. I stole a peek around the wall and watched her hurry up the stairs of another brownstone. The windows facing the street were covered by blinds but some light managed to bleed from the edges. After seeing no one on the street near enough to see me I moved stealthily up the stairs careful to control my breathing. I reached the top of the stairs and froze, listening for any sign someone inside had heard me.

The Kidnapping of Billy Buttons

Through the door I heard muffled voices speaking in low tones, but it didn't seem I'd been observed.

I moved closer to the door and took out a glass vial I kept in my coat from the inside pocket. I set one end of the vial against the door, the other end I placed next to my right ear.

The vial would amplify the voices on the other side. It was crude, but I'd used it before so I knew it worked well enough.

I listened intently. The voices had stopped. Had I been detected?

The sound of breaking glass was followed by an angry voice of a young male. A woman began to sob. I frowned and considered what I'd just heard. What was Helga doing in the middle of a domestic quarrel?

I decided to knock.

When the door flew open I found myself facing middle-aged man who was the spitting image of our new client. This could only be Skip Weezer's father.

**

I entered Edge's parents basement recreation room the next morning to find Edge seated in his Barcalounger eating his breakfast.

Of course for him cereal was also lunch, dinner, and in-between meal snacks so anytime I'd come in he'd have been eating Sugar Bombs, or Cherry Twists, or Captain Crisp, or any of the myriad of sugary breakfast cereals his parents kept stocked in the pantry.

His eyes were watching the television where the news was on. I walked to the sofa and sat down without saying anything.

"Hello, Razor," said Edge.

"Hi, Edge," I looked at the screen. Robert Weezer stood on the court house steps in Manhattan behind two lawyers in very expensive suits. One of the lawyers, a man with thinning steel gray hair, his face weathered and lined with emotion, his intense gray eyes studied the reporter asking him a question about the judges ruling this morning. Guy should have been an actor with a face and eyes like his.

"What's happening?" I asked.

Edge swallowed and said, "The judge ruled the bear must be returned to the present King of Rogberg."

"What about Mister Weezer?"

Edge shook his head. "No charges stuck to him provided he returns the bear within a week."

The Kidnapping of Billy Buttons

When Robert Weezer opened the door he asked me who I was and what I wanted. I explained his son hired me and Edge to find the person or persons who kidnapped Billy Buttons. I'm sure I sounded ridiculous but Mister Weezer ushered me inside anyway.

Helga was the crying woman, and a brunette named Tiffany (apparently Robert's new young girlfriend.) She explained the townhouse was her parents New York home and she let Robert use it. (She claimed her parents are the giants of the toothpaste business.)

"Think there'll be any issues?" Edge asked.

I shook my head. "No, now that they have the right bear it should be straight forward to FedEx it to Rogberg."

I had discovered the bears had been switched by Helga who was paid by Mister Weezer to steal the Rogberg bear. She removed the bear and replaced it with a more domestic 1940's era bear. Rare, but nowhere near the value of the Rogberg version, which would probably attract 1.2 million at auction if it ever came up for sale.

When Mister Weezer explained Rogberg agents were closing in on his bear he desperately wanted to spirit it out of the country to hide it a friends home in Bern, Switzerland.

This case was about love of nostalgia not money.

But what Robert Weezer didn't know was Helga was a Rogberg agent sent in undercover to work for various wealthy teddy bear collectors. But she had debts of her own (she's a bingo addict) so she saw an opportunity to take money from Weezer to kidnap the bear and she took it. (Weezer pays better than Rogberg.)

Helga was deported and now the bear would be returned to its rightful home.

My cell phone rang eliciting a glare from Edge. I answered it quickly.

I smiled when I read the screen saw who was calling. "Hi, Skip what's up?"

"Hi, Razor, I just wanted to call and say thank you."

"You're very welcome. Please thank your dad for the check. The money will help us buy a car, ability it slightly used." Truthfully very used.

"I'm glad. I'm going with dad to Rogberg."

"Sweet. Have fun."

"Thanks, Razor, I'll call you when I get back."

The Kidnapping of Billy Buttons

"Okay, kid, take it easy."I closed the phone after we said our goodbyes.

"Nice kid," observed Edge without looking in my direction.

"Yeah," I agreed. Skip had become a friend. When I revealed Helga's true identity his father apologized to Skip and promised to spend more time with him. Skip was very grateful I had taken the initiative to expose her as a Rogberg agent and that his father and he had started mending the fences of their relationship.

Mister Weezer explained he had been emotionally distant from his son after the sudden death of his wife, Skips mother. He wanted to rebuild their relationship. He'd even stopping seeing the young girl friend.

Maybe I took too much credit, but I discovered I really like Skip and was pleased for him. Was it because he was a nerd like me, or had a parental instinct suddenly surfaced in me? I have no idea, maybe a little of both.

One thing for sure, I was pleased Billy Buttons was going home.

Death by Clown

WHEN MY PARTNER, MORTON EDGE, entered his parents recreation room (the room serves double duty as the HQ of Razor and Edge Investigations, and the annual Winter in Hawaii Getaway and Cocktail Party hosted by Mr. and Mrs. Edge) he looked more distraught than I have ever seen him.

His face was blotchy and his normally clear hazel eyes were sunken, underneath were dark circles evidence of a serious lack of sleep. He moved across the room without speaking and sat in his well worn tan Barcalounger, the arms stained with spilled milk. Edge eats exclusively breakfast cereal, something that worries me sometimes, but he usually seems healthy enough. Today I was beginning to think the cereal diet had gotten the better of him.

Death by Clown

That was until he explained the reasons for his appearance.

"You OK?" I asked, glancing up from the laptop we usually keep stored in a closet in the recreation room for use in on-line research.

I was busy searching for the licensing requirements to allow us to procure locksmith tools which could come in handy in the course of our investigations. Locksmith tools certainly would have been useful when we had to recover my Aunt Sophie's parrot, Paulie, (yes, the name is a cliché, but Aunt Sophie's an old lady so she can name her parrot whatever she wants, whatya gonna do?) stolen from her ground floor apartment last year. That's a case I'll tell you about some time on our blog.

"No," he said without elaborating further.

His eyes flitted side to side and he sighed repeatedly. I closed the laptop and moved to the rickety kitchen chair beside his lounger. It was at times like this he needed a friend. Since Edge and I have been friends since grammar school I intended to be that friend.

I sat with my hands buried in my lap since Edge doesn't like to be touched, and spoke softly, "What's wrong?"

His watery gaze shifted to me.

It startled me when his eyes brimmed with tears. Edge never showed emotion. "My Aunt Cleo has been murdered."

*****

I came back with a six pack of diet Coke to find Edge sitting with the aluminum TV tray in front of his lounger, my laptop on the table. We keep the tray for Royce, leader of the Newspaper Boy League, who do early morning surveillance tasks for us while delivering their papers, to set his drink on while he makes his reports.

I know many of my regular readers will think I'm lying because Edge hates the modern world and its gadgets. He loathes the Internet so I'm the one who *surfs* the net when we need on-line information. To discover Edge using the laptop made my heart leap into my throat. I was so shaken I nearly dropped the soda cans. The world was about to end. I gasped and collapsed before I fainted onto the sofa.

Edge glanced at me from the corner of his eye then his eyes flitted back to the screen. The corners of his mouth curled slightly then settled into a grim line of determination to match his steely-eyed concentration on whatever he was looking at. "Don't worry, Jerome, I haven't slipped a wheel."

Death by Clown

Now I knew Edge wasn't well, he'd just used my real name. Next thing you know he'd start calling me Saperstein. "Edge," I said slowly, "it's me, Edge. Remember?"

Edge snorted. "Of course." Suddenly his face changed to wide smile and his eyes were bright with excitement. "Ah-ha! I found it!"

I was afraid to ask but I did anyway. "Found what?"

"The identity of the murderer."

A trickle of perspiration ran down the side of my face no doubt taking with it a trail of white makeup. Sometimes being Goth was a full time job.

Now I was really afraid to ask. What if he said it was a movie star or the CIA or Prince William? Then what do I do? When my partner and best friend since the third grade didn't speak for several seconds I decided to take the initiative. "So who is it?"

He looked over at me his face a mask of frightening calm, his eyes steady unblinking. "A clown killed my aunt."

Yup, he'd lost the battle to stay on this side of the reality pond. I decided to play along. "OK, Edge, what's our next move?" I mentally crossed my fingers hoping he wouldn't want to go after the clown.

Clowns scare the crap outta me, ever since my mom hired one for my tenth birthday party.

I shuddered at the memory of Bubbles the Clown's horrifying blotchy white makeup, his tobacco-stained yellow teeth, the purple fright wig, and the large red nose with the distended veins visible above blood-webbed, sunken eyes. And the smell of the stale booze hovered around him like a cloud of perverted perfume. (Even at the tender age of ten I knew what a booze hound and smoke jockey smelled like.)

Edge pointed at the screen. "We go to the scene of the crime."

I got up from the sofa then moved to stand beside his chair. Peering at the screen I saw a picture of an alley. The picture looked frozen until I saw a uniformed cop moved in from the left side of the picture. He was carrying what looked like a tackle box in his gloved left hand. Also, from the left a lean looking woman appeared dressed in blue jeans and a gray hoodie-style sweat shirt. The imagine wasn't in high def so it took me several seconds tro recognize her. She gave herself away when she pushed her glasses up her long nose with her left index finger. Molly. Molly Sharp, Edge's cousin.

Death by Clown

Molly was a crime scene technician, smart, opinionated, and so hot her mere presence boiled my water. I swallowed hard as the moisture in my mouth evaporated.

"Edge, where are you getting this footage?"

"It's a live feed," he said matter-of-factly.

A live feed? How did he know how to tap into a live feed from what was obviously a surveillance camera? And most importantly how did he get permission to view an active crime scene?

Before I could ask he offered an explanation. "My mom got me the access code to the camera system at my aunts building," Edge explained.

Since both his mother and father were New York county prosecutors they had access to every step of the investigative process. Problem was they weren't supposed to share this information outside the police and the prosecutor's office without permission. Edge's mother had just jeopardized her career. Of course since Cleopatra Blunt was her sister this was a personal situation, and I'm certain in this situation blood was thicker than the paper work she accidently-on-purpose forgot she needed to file to get the proper permission.

Problem for us was Detective Aimes was our primary window into the New York Police Department, and if our actions any way appeared to be skating on legal thin ice we could find ourselves on the outside looking in at lady justice. Illegal access to live video of an active crime scene certainly qualified as thin. This was no way to run a private detective agency if you plan to be in business for more than a year.

Since Edge was my friend I would go along with where ever this led us. Even if it meant a strict diet of bread and water at the crow bar hotel was in my future.

"You said you wanted to visit the crime scene. Do you mean together?"

Edge swiveled his lean frame in his lounger to face me. His eyes were steady, clear and determined. "Yes, we'll go together."

I shrugged trying to appear casual, but inside my guts were churning and my mind was racing. Edge never accompanied me on an investigation. Ever. I'm the leg man of our duo, it's my job to conduct the interviews, and buy the supplies (like his favorite breakfast cereal). Edge is the thinker, he reviews the information I gather then calls together the suspects and reveals the criminal.

Death by Clown

I worried Edge was too close to this investigation, and that there were too many family connections to allow him to be his usual subjective observer-self. If this case went south on us this could be the beginning of the end of Razor and Edge Investigations.

I paused to consider what file on the lap top contained my resume, and who might hire a failed Goth PI.

I went to the hall closet next to the door to the stairs that went up to the main floor of the house. After opening the closet door I selected my ankle length black leather coat with the orange and yellow flames design in the liner and put it on. I love this coat.

Edge pulled on his navy blue windbreaker and donned his mirrored sunglasses. I sniffed the air and detected the scent of Sugar Bombs, one his favorite cereals, and smiled to myself. At least her was still eating. I, on the other hand, was too nervous to eat for fear the food would come back up as fast as it went down.

"Where we going first?" I asked, after shrugging my shoulders so the coat with drape on my frame correctly.

"To the scene of the crime," he said with Sherlock Ian earnestness.

"Okay." Oh, brother, I thought. Is he going to be the king of all drama all the way along this trail of doom? I rolled my eyes. Now he's got me doing it.

*****

We arrived at the crime scene, the alley behind an apartment building on Erasmus Street in Brooklyn, in the most unusual way.

We came by taxi. Edge had never allowed me to use a taxi, explaining they cost far too much for our meager budget to weather. I tended to agree. But this case had a stranglehold on my partner so if it meant we had to blow the budget on extras then so be it. I like the old Edge far better than this new one. It was beginning to feel like I'd never known him at all.

They say the death of a loved one changes a person. No kidding! Molly and Edge's mothers were sisters to Cleopatra Blunt. I've always been amused the three sisters married, a Sharp, Edge and a Blunt. I guess tableware must run in the family tree. I expect the next generation will marry an Axe. (Sorry, bad jokes are my issue.)

I spotted Molly on her haunches near a dumpster about a hundred yards from where we stood behind the yellow crime scene tape strung across the entrance of the alley.

Death by Clown

Not that a bit of tape would stop us, but the large cop with arms the size of tree trunks glaring at us certainly would.

The alley itself was typical for this area of Brooklyn, only it was the cleanest alley I'd ever seen. I didn't detect the stench of even a single rotting banana peel, even though there were rolling dumpsters at regular intervals to the end of the alley which was a few city blocks distant.

"Hey, Molly," I called to get her attention.

She glanced over her shoulder at us. Her dark eyes narrowed and her brow wrinkled. She wasn't happy to see us. Now I wasn't so sure coming here was such a hot idea after all.

She rose to a standing position. She had on a clean suit and her hands were gloved. In one hand she held a clear evidence bag containing what looked like pottery fragments, in the other she held a pair of small tongs.

She sauntered toward us the scowl deepening with each step. Even in the clean suit and matching booties she was the sexiest woman on the planet. Her eyes were smoky and her lips were full and wet as if they'd just been licked. The bulky clean suit she had on covered her street clothes hiding her shapely figure, but my imagination was on full scan.

150

I envied knew the suit. As she approached I realized her attention was locked on Edge.

I glanced at Edge. He had a calm expression on his face and his hazel eyes were watchful but he didn't offer any of his usual observations.

"Hello, Morty," Molly said as she came up to us. Her voice has a husky edge to it that makes me (and I assume most red blooded males) weak at the knees.

My heart was pounding faster and I struggled to keep what I knew would be a stupid boyish grin off my face.

"Huh, hi, Molly," I said sheepishly. I wanted to slap my forehead with the palm of my hand. I must sound like a moron!

Her eyes shitted to me then back at Edge. "Yeah, hi," she said. "Morty, what are you and Jerome doing here?"

Edge cleared his throat then said, "Same thing you are, cus, trying to solve a murder."

The surprise registered in Molly's eyes, but quickly changed to annoyance. She glanced side to side to see if any of the uniformed cops were close enough to hear her. Satisfied they were far enough away she lowered her voice to a hoarse whisper as she said, "Who said I was doing anything but my job?"

Death by Clown

She slapped him on his left shoulder with the tongs. "And keep your voice down will ya?"

Edge arched a single eyebrow in that way he does when he knows he'd gained control of the interview. It always amazes me when he knows exactly where the weak spot is in a person and is able to exploit it.

"So what's going on, *cus*?" asked Edge. He had his hands stuffed into the pockets of his windbreaker and his eyes were locked with Molly's.

She pulled an iPhone from her suit pocket glanced at the screen then back into Edge's eyes. Molly's eyes were as hard and determined as Edge's. This family was a stubborn lot. From my many years of being around Edge's family I could spot the real thing in my sleep. Molly was all Edge...huh, I mean Sharp. Or is that Sharp-Edge?

"I'm going on break soon. Let's meet at Merry's Cafe on Rogers Avenue in say," she paused again to glance at her iPhone. "In ten minutes, OK?"

Edge glanced at me. I nodded. I knew the place. Decent coffee and somewhat edible food. Nothing fancy, but since it was after the lunch hour we should be able to talk with relatively little interruption.

"OK," Edge said. "See you there." With that he turned away and headed down the sidewalk away from the alley.

I smiled sheepishly at Molly. "Sorry, he can be so literal."

Molly smirked. "Yeah, I know. You should have seen him at the age of three."

"Oh?"

Molly scoffed, shook her head, and then walked away. At the other end of the alley I could see the coroners on site work trailer had been set up. Molly would change in there then meet us at the cafe.

I thought about offering to be her escort, but that would be so nerd so I turned and hurried after Edge.

*****

Fortunately the diner had a selection of breakfast cereals, some of which were even unhealthy, just like Edge likes them. By the time Molly entered and sat down I had a tuna fish on brown and a coffee, and Edge had a bowl of Corn Sugar Bombs in front of him.

"You're late," observed Edge in a matter-of-fact tone.

Molly smirked. "Yeah, and I see you're still eating breakfast cereal."

I couldn't help myself, I had to break this up. A woman was dead, and we had to find out who killed her and why.

153

"Listen you two," I began, "I know you guys have family issues, but we have to find out who murdered Cleo."

Edge stopped his spoon of cereal in mid-air and Molly stared at me with a pained expression on her face. Edge set the spoon back in the cereal bowl and shoved the bowl away from him. Obviously I'd just ruined his appetite. I must've raised my voice because the waitress, who was serving a table with two construction workers (they were dressed in dirty blue jeans and heavy, very scuffed up, work boots) seated at a table across the aisle from ours, had stopped in mid-pour from the glass coffee urn she was holding to turn and face us. She had a stunned expression on her face and her eyes as wide as dinner plates.

I smiled sheepishly at her. "We're writers," I offered as an explanation. "We're working on a TV pilot. Crime show," I added hoping that would suffice.

The waitress frowned, after refilling the two men's coffee cups she walked away with a harrumph of indignation. She obviously didn't believe me. I wouldn't have believed me either so I wasn't surprised by her reaction.

Molly lowered her voice to a whisper and leaned closer toward me making me want to pull away, but her eyes bore through me causing me to freeze in my seat. "Keep it down will, ya, Jerome, I could lose my job for even talking to you two about an active case. Normally," she added.

"But this is a relative," said Edge, so this circumstance is far different from normal as it gets.

The sadness crept in from the corners of Molly's eyes until I thought she would start to cry any second. I knew I better refocus us again and give this investigation a kick in its pants.

"How did Cleo die?" I asked.

Molly cast her watery gaze on me. She straightened her shoulders and cleared her throat. "She was struck on the head by an object."

"A clown?" I said, stealing a quick glance at Edge out of the corner of my eye. He sat passively watching Molly's reactions to my questions. I knew the look in his eyes, Edge was back on track, and his keen analytical mind was in full gear.

Molly looked at me surprise registering in her eyes. "Well, in a way, yes. She was struck on the head by a cookie jar shaped like the face of a clown that was dropped from a great height.

Death by Clown

The detectives suspect it was thrown off the roof of one of the buildings that border the alley."

"When did she die?"

Molly nodded, now fully in her element. "With no evidence of rigor and body temperature we suspect some time around midnight give or take an hour."

I frowned. "So your Aunt Cleo was wandering around in an alley at midnight, and a person, or persons, unknown who was on the roof of a building in Brooklyn, threw a clown head cookie jar that struck her in the head and killed her?" I shook my head. "That doesn't make a lot of sense...unless—" I stopped before I said what I was thinking. The last thing I wanted to do was add insult on top of tragedy. I knew Cleo was a fifth grade school teacher, and her husband, Rex made pretty good green at his job. (We called him Regimes Maximus since he's a big guy, and a longshoreman. Besides, it kind of fits with her name being Cleopatra.)

The last thing I needed to do was suggest the late Cleo was a lady of the streets.

Molly scowled at me. "My mother's sister isn't a hooker. What's the matter with you, Jerome? Has that makeup you wear affected your brain?"

Crap, I'd been outed. "No, of course not. That's not what I meant. I mean—"

156

Edge interrupted me saving my bacon for the frying pan. "He means, my dear cousin, did Aunt Cleo had no reason to be in this part of the city at that time of night."

Molly's eyes gradually softened. Finally she shifted her gaze to Edge. "Okay, let's assume she wasn't supposed to be here at midnight last night. Where was she supposed to be?"

A tight smile rose from the corners of Edge's mouth. "Exactly."

Molly frowned. "But I overheard one of the detectives talking on his cell to our uncle. After the call he said Uncle Rex told him he didn't know where his wife was last night, which makes sense because I used to visit auntie every Saturday night. Uncle Rex usually works the 9 p.m. to 9 a.m. shift on Saturdays."

"Then you saw her last night?" I interjected.

For the first time Molly avoided me by looking away. Her cheeks blushed a bright crimson. "Huh, no not this week. I had a date that...uhhhh...ran late."

I glanced at Edge who nodded, though I'm certain he had no idea what she was talking about. Not that Edge doesn't like women he just doesn't understand them.

"So we can eliminate you and Rex as suspects," said Edge.

Death by Clown

Molly's eyes shot to glare at Edge. I cringed inside.

Sometimes my partner's personality filters are on the lowest setting. He was oblivious to the fact he had just revealed his cousin was a potential suspect. I agreed with him, but I'd never have said it out loud. Inwardly I was relieved Molly had an alibi, but disappointed her romantic entanglements didn't include yours truly.

Edge continued as if Molly hadn't noticed. "Did Cleo tell you anything that might help us. Such as she had been threatened by someone, or was worried about anything?"

Molly shook her head but I could see in her eyes her mind was whirling, sorting through her memories of past conversations with Cleo, trying to make sense of her sudden death. Finally her shoulders slumped and I knew what she'd say before she said it. "No, I'm sorry. I can't think of any reason anyone would hurt Aunt Cleo. Everyone loved her. And as far as I know her marriage is, or was, rock solid."

Suddenly her eyes had that pained expression again. "Oh, my, Uncle Rex must be devastated."

Edge reached out and patted the back of hand. "The best thing we can do is find who killed her and ensure justice is served."

Molly eyes were watery when she looked into Edge's steady gaze. "Yes, Morty, you're right of course. But it's so shocking."

"Murder always is," I said.

Edge's forehead wrinkled and he had that faraway look in his eyes he gets when he's processing information. Finally he said, "If her marriage was rock solid as you say, and no one had threatened her, then either this is the work of a mad man, or mad woman, or it wasn't murder at all."

I stopped myself from scoffing. Like people throw random cookie jars from roof tops at midnight? Yeah, right. And besides you'd have to be the best cookie jar thrower on the planet to hit someone in an alley from ten five stories up. Cookie jars don't have laser targeting ya know.

Edge shook his head. "However, I seriously doubt this was an accident, and such an unusual weapon is hardly the choice for a murderer, even a random crazy one." Edge frowned deeper. "No, I suspect Cleo was murdered somewhere else then her body was dumped in the alley."

"But, Edge," I said, "they found fragments of the jar in the alley. We saw Molly picking them up."

Edge looked at Molly with an expression I knew well. He had solved the crime.

"My, dear cousin, this paramour of yours, what's his name?"

Molly scowled at Edge and crossed her arms over her bosom. My worst fears were about to be realized and no matter how I tried to mentally back peddle I couldn't escape the awful truth. Edge is never wrong. Ever. I've been down this road with Edge too many times not to know. Molly killed her aunt. Now all we needed was the why.

"That's none of your business, Morty," she said in a menacing tone.

Edge nodded. "You're absolutely correct, but I'm certain the police will want to know his name after I speak with Detective Aimes at the 2-2 and explain about the missing cookie jar."

Molly's eyes widened and her eyes flitted side to side then returned to lock eyes with Edge. Her voice was trembling and her face paled. "What cookie jar?"

"The one Aunt Cleo used to have on her kitchen counter that she used to serve me cookies from when we were kids. I suspect if we went to her house it would be gone. And I suspect Uncle Rex can confirm it was there recently."

He laid both arms flat on the table and leaned closer to Molly, his eyes were hard and his cheeks were flushed.

"Once the lab checks the fragments I suspect they'll find not all of the jar was in the alley, and they'll find residual dust on the floor of Aunt Cleo's kitchen when it shattered after you hit her with it. You, my dear cousin, are a murderer.

"Your insiders knowledge as a crime scene technician allowed you to stage the crime scene to appear to be the work of a random mad man. What you didn't anticipate was my insiders knowledge of a certain cookie jar."

He paused and leaned back against his chair. "Now I want to know why."

Molly regarded him for several seconds with narrow eyes, her jaw set in determination. I worried she'd stick to her alibi, but if she came clean and confessed, Edge would put in a good word for her with his mother and father, and with the police. That way she might have a shot at a murder-in-the-second plea bargain.

Suddenly Molly's shoulders slumped and she spoke in a whisper. "When did you know?"

Edge's lips formed a grim line. "As soon as we arrived at the crime scene and I saw the pottery fragments."

Molly chuckled grimly and she shook her head. "I knew you'd be trouble when you showed up."

Death by Clown

"Shall we go see the detectives?" Edge asked. Molly nodded and her head slumped forward, but she remained silent. Good idea under the circumstances.

When we got up from the table. I glanced at the two construction workers who had eyes wide as saucers. "Gonna be some show," I said cheerfully. "Monday's at 8, 7 central." They nodded in unison.

Man, I'm good.

*****

The next morning when I arrived at Edge's parent's basement I found him reading a book on the Spanish Armada. As is his usual practice he sat in his barolounger with a can of lemon lime soda on the end table next to his chair.

"Hi, Edge," I said and went to retrieve the laptop from the hall cupboard. Today I was planning on catching up on my blog. I couldn't push myself to write about Cleo's murder yet, but I had a piece about a squirrel hunt I thought might be interesting. A grunt was his only response. he didn't bother to look up.

After opening the computer case I set up the lap top on the scarred coffee table then plugged it in. while it booted up I thought I'd engage Edge about yesterday's events.

"Edge, when did you really know Molly killed your aunt?"

He looked up from his book then closed it and set in on the table next to his can of soda. "I suspected her when I saw the video from the alley."

"Then why did you have to go with me to the alley?"

Edge crossed his legs at the ankle and frowned. "Molly's family. I needed to be sure. And I didn't think she'd come here knowing I would see through any deception from someone I've known much of my life."

"OK, but, Edge, why did she kill Cleo?"

"I'm not sure we'll ever know with absolute certainty." He paused and I could see by his expression, and in his eyes he was considering all the possibilities. "It could be Molly owed her money, or they argued and it got out of control."

I nodded. "You could be right." Something I knew that Edge didn't was Molly had been having an affair with Rex. Detective Aimes told me privately. Edge will never know, at least I won't tell him.

"I'm thinking of calling the blog death by clown. What do ya think?"

Edge nodded slowly. "Sounds reasonable. But please wait a while before you post it."

I nodded. And I'd leave out certain details.

About the Author

International selling author, Russ Crossley, writes science fiction and fantasy, and mystery/suspense.

The second book in his science fiction satire series, *Revenge of the Lushites*, released by 53rd Street Publishing in the fall of 2013, is available now in e-book and trade paperback.

Several of his short stories have appeared in anthologies from 53rd Street Publishing, WMG Publishing, Pocket Books, and St. Martins Press. His short story, available now at Over My Dead Body online Mystery magazine, is titled *Instrument of Justice*.

Contact him on Facebook, Twitter, or his website www.russcrossley.com.

Other books by the Author

Razor and Edge Mysteries
The Kidnapping of Billy Buttons
String of Pearls
Death by Clown
Beggin' For Murder
Ragged Ice
The Grand Central Mystery
A Strange Case of Undead Murder

Jazz Stiletto Mysteries
A Day Without Sunshine
Skullduggery
Instrument of justice (first published in Over My Dead
Body online mystery magazine)

The Amanda Dark paranormal mysteries
Hook Island
Grind Manor
Moonrise Diner

The Trudy Wilson Mysteries
Bad Loyalty
Shear Murder
Buzzcut coming in 2015

Novels
Attack of the Lushites
Revenge of the Lushites

My Zombie Prince
Antique Virgin
The Fire In Their Hearts
with R.S. Meger (from Champagne Books)
Zomopolis
The Last Serial Killer

Short Stories
Countdown
Shoeless Moe
Round Up At The Burger Bar:
The Story of Trixie Pug, Parts 1, 2, 3, 4, 5, 6, 7, 8, 9
Five Minutes
Blossom Queen, Barbarian
The Secret
The Family Line
End of the Flies
Death by Magic
The Penguin Sleeps With The Fishes
Only The Worthy
Hero For A Day
End of Empire
Strange Bedfellows
Big Business
A Perfect Crime
The Wise Guy and The Pirates
In Search of the Perfect Cup
T.I.N. Men
The Legend of G and the Dragonettes
The Incredible Mr. Fix-It
Lock Stock and Barrel
Divided Loyalties

Cave of Wonders
A Family Empire
Until We Meet Again
Dragon Rising
Solitary Man
The Keel Mountain Conspiracy
Angel on My Shoulder
Heroes of Old
The Great Bicycle Race
Tikka's Big Day
"My Partner the Zombie" —
Hungry For Your Love Anthology
(St. Martin's Press)
Big Hairy Deal
One Red Shoe
A Bad Day in Lunden Texas
Bloody Betty, Queen of the Pirates
Mirror Image
Dangerous Waters
Cape Disappointment
Boomerang
The Watcher of Wayburn Street
The Apprentice
Drip!
A Beautiful Friendship and The Parrot of Doom
Robine's Diary
The Christmas Club
Loose Ends
Splatter Pattern
It Takes Two
Lexicon

Anthologies
Tales of Urban Fantasy
Five Tales of Bizarre Detectives
Tales of Mystery and Suspense
Tales of Weird Fantasy
Spies, Detectives, & Heroes
Tales of Twisted Crime
Tales of The Unexpected
Tales From Space
10 by Russ Crossley
Round Up At The Burger Bar: The Story of Trixie Pug,
Parts 1- 5 The Beginning
Worlds of Science Fiction and Fantasy
More Tales of Mystery and Suspense
Ladies of the Jolly Roger
Justice Served
Love Stories
Ladies of the Jolly Roger with R.S. Meger
The Adventures of Razor and Edge:
Five Tales From The Quirky Detective Team

Non-Fiction
The Writers Tools - The Synopsis

Also available from 53rd Street Publishing at your favorite online retailer or book store,. The book is available in print and ebook formats.

The first book in the Trudy Wilson Mystery series

A murder in Canada thrusts hairdresser Trudy Wilson into the middle of a web of conspiracy that threatens to send her friend, biker Bruce Carstairs, to prison forever. loyalty drives her to rush to his side to get to the truth. but loyalty can be deadly...